Emmaline and the Fluffles

by

JJ McGeester

To Mrs Kessler's 5th Graders
You are awesome! I hope
you enjoy this book.
Read More! Write More!
JJ

www.jjmcgeester.com

ISBN: 1547154217
ISBN-13: 978-1547154210

First Edition

For Emmaline

Table of Contents

Preface from the Author

Dear Reader,

I am writing this letter from the back of an ostrich. You probably haven't received many letters written from the back of an ostrich. (I haven't written more than five in my entire life, maybe six). I'm fleeing an angry swarm of butterflies—I don't have time to explain, something about a rigged chicken race. Regardless, you should realize this is important. If someone writes to you from the back of an ostrich while fleeing an angry swarm of butterflies, you had better pay attention.

I will say it once: do not read this book. You may be thinking, *Oh look! A cute, happily-ever-after fairy tale with a happy princess and a happy knight and happy little bunnies that hop around and nibble happy little rose petals.* Which, of course, would be wrong. The story on the following pages is a tale of all-encompassing misery and the end is anything but happy. So no, a happily-ever-after fairy tale this is not.

I am attaching this warning letter to Ronaldo, my fastest chicken. My wish is for Ronaldo to hop, cluck, and peck his way back to my publisher's office before it's too late to stop them from printing this book. Hopefully, the publisher gets this letter, reads it, and burns the manuscript, instead of adding it to the front of the book and splashing the words "Preface from the Author" on the top.

Sincerely,

The Stranger

EMMALINE, THE QUEEN'S YOUNG ASSISTANT, stood alone and picked raspberries in the grassy field at the edge of the forest. Emmaline was small for her age. She was generous, kind, and loved by all the townspeople. Her long hair fell about her face playfully, and she preferred skipping to walking when outdoors. The raspberries were plump, red, and so tender that when you put one in your mouth, it simply dissolved into sweet nectar so delicious you'd close your eyes, lean your head back, and sigh. Emmaline placed a raspberry on her tongue. She, like you would have, closed her eyes, leaned her head back, and sighed.

When she opened her eyes, a woman stood in front of her. The woman had simply appeared as if she were a small tree that had grown in the raspberry patch in the time it took to eat a single raspberry.

"Oh my!" said Emmaline. "You startled me."

The stranger standing in front of Emmaline was tall, slender, and wore a tattered black cloak which was muddy on both the bottom hem and the end of the sleeves. Her bony fingers clutched a wooden staff with an ornate carving of ivy leaves circling up to the top where they entwined a gray stone. The woman's shoulders sagged. Her black hair was streaked with gray and clung to her worn and tired face. A scar traced its way from slightly above her left eye, down her cheek, and ended just under her nose. She looked exhausted in all aspects except one: her eyes. The eyes darted from side to side before settling on Emmaline.

"Oh. I'm so sorry dear. I didn't mean to frighten you."

The woman took a step forward with her right foot then dragged her left foot forward to meet it, all while leaning on the wooden staff. Her eyes stared at the young girl.

"Could you tell me where I am? I'm afraid I got a bit turned around in the woods."

"This is Zantavia. That's Queen Iliana's castle over there," replied Emmaline, pointing over her shoulder. On the far side of the field, spires and towers and smoke from cooking fires rose in the sky. Three mountains, "the three sisters" the locals would say, watched over the castle.

"Zantavia you say. Hmm. . . . I hear it is a very nice kingdom." The woman looked at the castle in the distance, thought for a second or two, then looked back at Emmaline. "Well, it looks lovely from here. I would like to see it someday. But, unfortunately, I must be on my way."

She took a step, lost her balance, and tottered forwards. The woman reached out a bony hand and grabbed Emmaline's shoulder. Her fingers dug into Emmaline's skin. She leaned forward and coughed. Her breath came in short bursts.

"Are you OK?" said Emmaline, who grabbed the woman's elbow and helped her stand.

"I just—" but the woman was overcome with coughing and couldn't continue.

"Let me take you back to the castle. You don't look well. Queen Iliana will know what to do."

The mysterious woman looked down, as if she were thinking over a great problem written in the raspberry leaves, then said, "Yes. Maybe that's a good idea. Maybe today's the day I see Zantavia."

Emmaline held out her arm and led the woman down the path towards the castle.

As she walked, the woman stood up a little straighter. Her eyes continued to dart about, examining the fields and the woods and the raspberry patch, the path towards the castle, and, lastly, the side of Emmaline's head. And then the mysterious woman grinned.

Queen Iliana
Meets the Stranger

LESS THAN AN HOUR LATER, Emmaline and the mysterious woman sat outside Queen Iliana's meeting room. The Queen was everything you'd want from a queen; she was regal, intelligent, compassionate, and warm-hearted; she was stern when she needed to be, yet fair, and was always ready with a smile or an encouraging word. She and Emmaline resembled each other, and although the Queen didn't have any children of her own, Emmaline was practically her daughter as the Queen raised Emmaline after the disappearance of the girl's parents years ago which, I hate to say, is a story not meant for this book. Emmaline loved Queen Iliana and Queen Iliana loved her.

Queen Iliana was also loved by the townspeople (some of whom are mentioned below but whom we'll meet more fully later in the story). Inside the meeting room, a discussion between the Queen and several townspeople was coming to an end.

"So, let me just be certain we haven't missed anything for the party," said Queen Iliana. "Baker, you will make a cake—one of your famous seven-layer cakes I hope. Jeweler, you will finish making the new chandelier. Hervé will manage the cooking and Emmaline will be in charge of serving. Celine is in charge of the music and Davinda will perform on the trapeze. Bella will take care of cleanup, unless, that is, you'd rather try to set the world brick-stacking record. I hear there's a fellow in Beckinsdale who can hold five hundred bricks over his head."

Bella, a world-class bodybuilder and the strongest person in the kingdom, chuckled. "No, Your Highness. As much as I'd like to show them who's the strongest, the idea of stacking bricks over my head and holding them in the air seems rather silly, although I'm certain I could do more than five hundred."

"Agreed," said Queen Iliana as she scratched a line through the last item on her list. "I guess that does it. Queen Pixoratta and the Fluffles leave their home tomorrow, which means they will arrive here in less than two weeks, giving us plenty of time to prepare. When they arrive we'll have the biggest celebration Zantavia has ever seen. I'm so excited! Thank you all for helping."

The townspeople stood, mulled about briefly, chatted a bit more, then walked out the door. Queen Iliana said her final goodbyes and spied Emmaline sitting in the hallway next to the mysterious woman wearing a dirty black cloak. Not looking at Emmaline, but rather at the mysterious person hunched over in the chair next to her, the Queen said, "Emmaline, so good to see you. How was the berry picking?"

"Good, Your Majesty. The raspberries are just about perfect."

The Queen tilted her head at the stranger then looked at Emmaline.

"Oh, yes. Queen Iliana, let me introduce you to. . . . Heavens! I don't even know your name." Emmaline's face reddened.

The stranger coughed a dry hacking cough and struggled to stand before a second coughing fit forced her to sit back down. She weakly held out a hand and shook the Queen's hand with the same warmth a wet rag might shake a squid.

"Bagalon, Your Highness. My name's Bagalon. I apologize for not standing up, but I haven't been feeling so well lately. I was walking through the field when Emmaline rescued me. I was extremely lucky to find her."

"Indeed you were," said the Queen, raising an eyebrow. "What brings you to Zantavia, Bagalon?"

"Ah, well, you see, I'm on my way to visit my Aunt Polly in Blenko. She's quite sick you know. Flagmatoid strombisis, very serious—deadly even—and I wanted to go see her and pay my regards before . . . before . . ." Bagalon burst into tears. She sobbed as her body shook.

"There, there. Bagalon. Take a deep breath. I'm sorry to hear about your Aunt Polly," said Iliana. "Blenko is quite a ways from here. Especially if you aren't feeling healthy. You should stay here tonight."

"Oh, but I can't! It's my dear Aunt Polly, and nothing could ever keep me from seeing her in her time of need. Dear, sweet Aunt Polly. I really should be going. I can't bear the thought of not seeing her." Bagalon stood and was immediately taken over by another fit of coughing. She leaned on her staff with both hands.

"Please. Bagalon. You're in no shape for traveling. Rest here. Get a good night's sleep. We'll feed you and, if you're feeling up to it, you can continue your journey in the morning after breakfast."

"Well, I guess I could spend one night here. But I really must be going first thing tomorrow morning. I'll be gone before breakfast. I don't want to be a bother."

"Nonsense! You'll be no bother at all. See how you feel in the morning and we can decide about breakfast then. Emmaline, run ahead and pour a hot bath and have Cook prepare a nice soup for Bagalon. We'll meet you at the guest chambers."

Emmaline nodded and raced down the hall.

Queen Iliana extended her elbow, which Bagalon held for support, and the two walked down the hall slowly. Iliana would stop whenever her new guest was overcome with a coughing fit.

"So, Bagalon, where do you call home?"

Bagalon's eyes darted from side to side. "Pentuxet, Your Highness. I've lived there all my life."

"Really? It's such a small town we rarely see anyone from there. The Earl of Pentuxet is a good friend of mine. I'm sure you must know him."

"Ah, well, when I said I was from Pentuxet, what I meant was I was *born* there, but then we moved away when I was just a little baby, so I don't really know anyone from there."

"I see. So, where is home these days?"

"Oh, a little here. A little there. I tend to travel a lot. I don't really stay in one place too long. I was in Panshaw last week."

"Ah. That explains it. I was wondering how you could end up here. Blenko is in the opposite direction."

The Queen and Bagalon arrived at a door leading into the guest chambers, where they found Emmaline waiting.

"Here is your room. I hope you have a restful evening and I will see you in the morning."

Bagalon nodded then looked into the lavish bedroom. A large bed, covered with soft blankets and pillows, sat on one wall. Ornate drapes hung on either side of a wide window. In the center of the room, steam rose from a claw-foot bathtub.

"Oh! This is wonderful!" said Bagalon. Her face lit up. She stood up a little straighter, then stopped and hunched back down.

"Is there anything else you might need?" asked Emmaline.

"No no! This is perfect." Bagalon pushed past Emmaline. "Thank you. Goodnight." Bagalon slammed the door shut, leaving Emmaline and the Queen in the hallway. She leaned the staff against a wall, twisted the key in the lock, clapped both her hands together, and tried to suppress a giggle. She skipped over to the table, pulled her tattered dress over her head, and slowly lowered herself into the steaming bath. She held the soup bowl in her hands and slurped.

"Oh, I could get used to this!" she said.

In the hallway, Queen Iliana looked at Emmaline and said, "Keep your eye on her, Emmaline. That woman can't be trusted. I want Bagalon out of the castle first thing in the morning."

Breakfast

THE NEXT MORNING, WELL BEFORE BREAKFAST, Emmaline woke up, got dressed, and walked down to the guest bedroom, where she found the door open, the bed unmade, and Bagalon's tattered dress discarded on the floor. There was, however, no sign of Bagalon. Then Emmaline went to the Queen's bedroom, which, although neater, also showed no signs of its occupant. Finally, Emmaline walked down the hallway to the dining room, where she found Queen Iliana as well as Bagalon, who wore a new dress.

"Good morning, Emmaline. Bagalon here was just telling me how she can't stay for breakfast."

"I was? Oh. Yes. I must go to see Aunt Penelope."

"Penelope? Yesterday you said were going to see Aunt Polly."

"Oh, yes! Well, Aunt Penelope is Polly's sister. I really must be going so I can help Penelope take care of poor Aunt Polly. I can't leave her alone in her condition."

"I'm sure Aunt Polly will be happy to see you. Emmaline, escort Bagalon out of the castle, so she can get to her Aunt Polly as fast as possible."

Emmaline offered her arm, but Bagalon, instead of taking it, turned towards the Queen and said, "Well, I guess I could stay for some tea. Just a little bit. If it's not too much trouble."

"What about Aunt Polly's illness?"

"Oh, yes. Well, decaying diopsis actually takes a while before it gets too bad. I'm sure she'll be fine."

"I thought you said Aunt Polly had flagmatoid strombisis."

"Ah! Yes, well, see she has decaying diopsis *and* flagmatoid strombisis. So it's very, very bad. But the diopsis actually slows down everything else, so she'll be fine for a little while."

"Ah. And here I thought it was a grave issue."

"Very grave, but not as urgent as you might think."

Queen Iliana tilted her head back and examined the mysterious woman standing in front of her.

"Well, if you think you have the time, I'm sure we can share a bit of tea. Emmaline, would you go into the kitchen and bring our guest some tea?" Queen Iliana sat down at the head of the dining table and Bagalon sat to her right, in Emmaline's usual chair.

Emmaline walked towards the swinging doors which lead into the kitchen.

"With milk!" said Bagalon, "and three scoops of sugar!"

Queen Iliana looked over her guest. "I notice you're not coughing today, Bagalon, and your limp seems to have gone away as well."

"Oh, well, um, yes. I'm feeling a little bit better," Bagalon said as she covered her mouth and coughed lightly. She grabbed her staff in her right hand. "At least I have this to help me get where I'm going."

Emmaline pushed the door open and entered the kitchen. Hervé was busy preparing the day's meals. Emmaline filled a pot with water, set it over the stove, and chatted with Hervé and the servants while the water heated. A minute later, the water was boiling. Emmaline grabbed two teacups, added tea leaves, and filled the cups with hot water. She let the tea soak in the water for a bit, removed the leaves, placed the cups on a tray, poured milk and three spoons of sugar into one, then turned to walk back through the swinging door to the dining room but froze in her footsteps. From underneath the door, a bright red light glowed, as if the room beyond had been filled with a dying sunset. Emmaline pushed on the door and was immediately struck by a dry heat. A faint trace of smoke hovered around Queen Iliana's head then drifted away like ghosts in the morning.

As the door opened, Bagalon, who had been standing, quickly sat down and rested her staff against the table. She covered her mouth and coughed quietly.

"Here is your tea, ladies. I was wondering if—Queen Iliana, are you OK?"

The Queen's mouth hung open. Her eyes were glassy and stared at nothing in particular on the far wall.

"Pretty stone . . . ," she said.

"I'm sorry?" said Emmaline.

"Very . . . pretty . . . ."

Emmaline grabbed Queen Iliana by the shoulders. "Queen Iliana? Can you hear me?"

Queen Iliana blinked several times and slowly turned her head towards Emmaline. She blinked again, shook her head, and said, "What did you say, Emmaline?"

"Can you . . . well . . . can you hear me?"

"Of course."

"Are you feeling OK?"

"I'm fine. Why?"

"Well, you seemed a little, confused I guess."

"Whatever gave you that idea?" The Queen took both cups of tea and placed one in front of Bagalon. Then, as if a thought had suddenly struck her, added, "Oh, Emmaline, have Hervé make up an extra plate for Bagalon. She'll be having breakfast with us."

"What about Aunt Polly?"

"I *insist* Bagalon stays for breakfast," said Queen Iliana.

"Well, if you insist," said Bagalon. "You are the queen. But only for breakfast. After that, I really must be on my way."

Bagalon's wrinkly lips twisted into a smile as Emmaline returned to the kitchen to tell Hervé the news.

The Happiness Law

BAGALON STAYED FOR BREAKFAST. And, as it turned out, she stayed for lunch, dinner, and three meals the following day. And then three more the day after that. When asked about Aunt Polly, she would reply that the illness was grave, but not that grave, and her cousin or brother or uncle or neighbor with the small dog could take care of Polly for a little while.

Queen Iliana, who had once said, "I want Bagalon out of the castle first thing in the morning," somehow was no longer in a hurry to have the strange woman leave. On the contrary, at any mention of leaving, the Queen would insist Bagalon stay. The two spent all their waking hours together, appearing to be lifelong friends even though they had only met a few days prior. On several occasions, Emmaline tried to talk with the Queen privately to discuss her concerns about the mysterious stranger, but somehow Bagalon would appear and change the conversation or distract the Queen, leaving Emmaline alone with her suspicions.

Most concerning was Queen Iliana's health. It started to deteriorate. She looked tired; her eyes sagged; puffy bags formed under her eyelids; her walking slowed; and she often was confused, not hearing Emmaline, or only hearing her after saying an odd collection of words, like, "swirly red clouds," "I insist," or "pretty stone." At the same time, Bagalon's health markedly improved. She walked without a limp, though she still walked with her staff, and her coughing was all but gone.

Lastly, and most oddly, on more than one occasion Emmaline smelled a faint whiff of dry smoke, which came and went so quickly she couldn't be sure if she really smelled it or if her mind was playing tricks on her. Sometimes she noted the room felt warmer but again wasn't really sure.

On one particular day, Queen Iliana felt particularly unwell. She lay in her bed even though the sun had risen and everyone was out and about. Her forehead glistened with sweat. Emmaline sat on the edge of the bed, wrung out a wet towel, and rested it on Queen Iliana's forehead.

"Bagalon, what do you think is wrong with Queen Iliana?" asked Emmaline.

"Maybe her mattress isn't comfortable," said Bagalon, who stood in front of the Queen's closet and admired her collection of fine dresses.

"She's sick," said Emmaline.

"Maybe she was poisoned," said Bagalon. She looked at Emmaline's face, saw the shock and terror flow through it, and laughed. "Oh Emmaline, I'm just kidding!" Bagalon turned back to the dresses.

"Your Majesty, is everything OK? Is there anything I can do for you?" asked Emmaline.

"Emmaline, you're too sweet." The Queen reached out a clammy hand and patted the back of Emmaline's fingers. "I just need some rest is all. Bagalon can take care of me. Maybe you can make sure everyone in the kingdom is happy. I haven't been able to check in with them lately."

"I distinctly heard some people say they *weren't* happy," said Bagalon, turning a dress in her hand.

"What's that?" asked Queen Iliana. She struggled to sit up, couldn't, and slouched back down.

"Just last night, I distinctly heard someone say, 'No, I'm not happy at all.'" Bagalon held a dress up and looked in the mirror. She smoothed the fabric and tilted her head. She swirled to the left and then to the right. Bagalon shrugged, hung the dress back in the closet, pulled out another, and continued to spin and twist in front of the mirror.

"Someone in my kingdom is not happy?"

"I hate to be the one who brings you the bad news, but yes," Bagalon agreed. "At least one person is unhappy, and maybe more. You probably should do something about it right away. Unhappiness is like a disease—if you don't stop it at once, it will spread from one person to another."

"Really, Bagalon? What can I do?" The Queen coughed slightly, as if her throat was filled with smoke.

Emmaline shifted on the bed. "Your Majesty, let me check and see if there is anything to be concerned about. I'm sure it's nothing."

Bagalon lowered the dress in front of her. "That will take too long. If one person is unhappy, soon another will be unhappy, then another, and then everyone will be unhappy. What I would suggest, Your Highness, is to make a law: everyone must be happy at all times. You're the queen, after all. It wouldn't take but a second."

Emmaline's face twisted underneath her brow.

The Queen looked at Bagalon. "A law?"

"I don't think we need—" said Emmaline.

"Yes. A law." Bagalon hung up the dress, picked up her wooden staff, and crossed back to the bed. She held the staff in such a way that the stone at the top hovered in front of the Queen's eyes. "If I were you, I'd *insist* everyone be happy in my kingdom."

A sudden change came over Queen Iliana. Her eyes glassed over. The muscles in her face eased and her eyebrows relaxed into a gentle curve. She spoke quietly, slowly, as if she were in a faraway place, forming words and hoping the wind would take them to their final destination.

"A law. . . . No unhappiness. . . . Everyone in kingdom happy. . . . At all times, must be happy. Emmaline, put . . . notice on oak tree."

"Wait. I'm confused," said Emmaline. "You want to make a *law* that everyone has to be happy?"

"A law. Yes. . . . Everyone . . . happy," said Queen Iliana. She closed her eyes. Her breathing slowed and she fell asleep.

Emmaline looked at Bagalon. "I don't think that Queen Iliana really wants to make a law insisting everyone be happy. The kingdom has never needed a law about happiness before. I think I should wait for her to wake up. It's just the fever talking."

"Tut! Your job is not to think, Emmaline! It is to do the Queen's bidding. And right now she bids that you make it known to all the townspeople that they are required by law to be happy at all times. Put an official notice on the oak tree in the center of town. Queen Iliana *insisted* on it."

"But that seems silly. I think we should—"

"Ah ah ah!" said Bagalon, waving a finger at Emmaline. "Don't think, Emmaline. You just run along. This new law will make everyone happy, including Queen Iliana."

"Well, I guess so. I do hope she feels better soon." Emmaline smoothed the blankets and then brushed a lock of hair from Queen Iliana's face before walking out the door.

Bagalon stroked the stone at the end of her staff as if she were petting a cat. "And as for me, I'm just happy Queen Iliana wasn't poisoned."

Happiness Descends
on the Kingdom

THE NEXT DAY, THE TOWNSPEOPLE GATHERED around the large oak tree and read the announcement Emmaline tacked to the tree. Years had passed since a new law had been introduced—something about taking chickens into taverns. Mrs. Gertgen was the only one old enough to remember when that law was passed, but for the life of her she couldn't remember why chickens were (or was it weren't?) allowed to sit at a bar and enjoy a drink.

The announcement stated the following:

> # ATTENTION!
>
> By order of Her Majesty Queen Iliana, it is hereby decreed that all residents, at all times, now and forthwith, for time eternal, be happy.

"What do you suppose it means?" said the Jeweler.

"I think it means we have to be happy all the time," answered the small man with the round glasses.

"*Everyone*?"

"It looks that way. Yes, I would say everyone."

"All the time?" asked the Baker's Husband.

"Well, it says 'at all times,' so yes. I think so."

"Well, I'm happy when I'm eating my wife's cookies, so it's easy for me," the Baker's Husband responded.

"And I love making cookies for you too, my little Snookie-Bear," said the Baker.

"Well, I love my work too," added Humungo, the town blacksmith, "but not all the time. Last week I smashed my thumb between a hammer and a horseshoe. It's still black and blue, and I can assure you I was *not* happy when that happened."

"Then you better not hit your thumb again," said the small man with the round glasses. "If you do, you'll be breaking the law. That is unless you come up with a way to smash your thumb that makes you happy."

"Not a chance," Humungo replied.

More discussions followed. And even more questions.

For the next two days, the kingdom was abuzz with talk of the new law, but by the third day conversations returned to the weather and the daily activities in town. Gertie thought the rutabagas would be ready for harvest before too long. Little Jonas's birthday was coming up soon and Clarence's horse was found down by Mr. Tamernick's barn, yet again. Old Man Quindle was still alive, but it would be good to check on him. After a week, the happy little town was back to normal and the townspeople stopped thinking about the new law.

An Insistence on Happiness

INSIDE THE CASTLE'S GREAT DINING ROOM, Emmaline and Bagalon sat across from the Queen, who slumped in her chair and pushed a spoon through a small bowl of soup. Her hair hung in clumps and she wore the same nightgown she had worn for the past two days.

"Emmaline, did you post the new law on the oak tree?" Queen Iliana asked.

"Yes, Your Highness."

"Did the townspeople see it?"

"Yes, they did."

"What did they say? Are they happy?"

"Well, I think they are a bit confused."

"Confused? Why?"

"Well, Your Highness, I think there is some confusion as to *how* happy they need to be and for how long."

"I guess I'm not really sure, Emmaline. How do you measure happiness?"

Bagalon waved an arm through the air. "You don't *measure* happiness! Everyone needs to be *completely* happy all the time! Isn't that right, Emmaline?" Bagalon took a large bite of mutton and mashed potatoes.

Emmaline fidgeted in her chair. "Well, the Blacksmith said something about smashing his thumb with a hammer and not being happy."

Queen Iliana stared at the cold soup in front of her.

Bagalon swallowed the mutton and washed it down with a large mouthful of red wine. "Iliana, this is a wonderful kingdom, and you are without a doubt the best Queen in the world, the absolute best. Don't get me wrong, but . . . there are some unhappy people out there. Why, just this morning I saw a baby crying and her mother was crying too. I don't think it was because they were happy, either. I'm not sure, but if I were you, I'd *insist* everyone follow the law." Bagalon leaned in over the Queen as she said the word *insist*.

Queen Iliana sat upright in her chair. She waved her spoon in the air. "I *insist* everyone follow the law! I *insist* everyone is happy!" She slammed her fist on the table. The plates jumped and the soup leaped in the air. "Emmaline! Bagalon! Make certain everyone is happy. Right away!"

"Absolutely, Your Highness." Emmaline stood up from her unfinished meal and hurried to the door. She looked back to find Bagalon still sitting at the table, filling her face with large bites of mutton and mashed potatoes. "Aren't you coming, Bagalon?"

Bagalon finished the last bite on her plate, licked each of her fingers one at a time, making a loud *schlopp* sound as the end of each finger popped out of her mouth. "I'll catch up with you in a minute, Emmaline. I need to talk with Iliana about something, um, private." Bagalon grabbed her staff and walked around the table.

Emmaline nodded, curtsied toward Queen Iliana, and left the two women alone in the dining room. As she turned and continued down a hallway, she could make out the sound of Bagalon's voice, some murmuring, and the sound of what she thought was a chair falling over, but she wasn't sure. A bright red light shimmered from behind her, but when she turned around to look, the hallway was empty.

The Unhappy Jeweler

BAGALON AND EMMALINE WALKED through town. Shopkeepers welcomed the ladies into their stores with a "Good morning! How are you this beautiful day?" Farmers waved from their fields. Everyone was friendly, smiling, and happy—just like they had always been.

The two passed in front of the Jeweler's shop where necklaces and bracelets gleamed in the windows. Sparkling gems made from secret metallic powders blazed in the reflected sunlight. Swirling colors ebbed and flowed on bracelets in the display cases, as if the jewelry were alive. There was a reason the Jeweler was world-renowned: her designs were simply astonishing.

"Did you hear that shout, Emmaline? It sounded like someone was upset!" Bagalon exclaimed. She turned and clapped her hands together. "It came from inside the Jeweler's store."

Bagalon opened the door and raced in. She looked around the room. Cases held a dizzying assortment of necklaces, bracelets, and earrings. On the wall, a certificate proclaimed *First Place, Dynamic Designs, Pendant Division*. Next to it hung a painting of the Jeweler arm-in-arm with Queen Iliana, who wore a sumptuous green and yellow pendant.

"Hello! Is anyone here?"

"I'm in the workshop!" a voice shouted from the back.

Bagalon navigated through the store, opened a door, and entered the Jeweler's workshop. Emmaline followed behind.

"Is everything OK?" asked Bagalon. "I thought I heard a shout."

"Oh, that was me," said the Jeweler, on her hands and knees next to a workbench. "I was working on my latest project—a dolphin pendant made of diamonds, silver, and an iridescent metal. I'm trying to make it look like the dolphin is floating on water," said the Jeweler.

"Ooh! That sounds lovely," said Emmaline.

"Yes, well it would be, except my cat, Mr. Pickles, knocked over the jar holding my iridescent powder. He spilled tiny flecks of metal all over."

Emmaline looked around the workshop. Sparkling, shimmering metallic dust covered the table, floor, and Mr. Pickles the cat, who looked like a sleepy shiny fish lying on the windowsill, licking iridescent powder from his paws.

"Now I have to pick up all the powder—a single grain at a time. If you try to sweep it up, it just sticks to the broom."

"My heavens! That is terrible! Here, let me help you," said Emmaline. She bent down and started to pick up grains of iridescent powder, one at a time, and put them in the jar.

"Yes," agreed Bagalon, who stood looking down at the Jeweler and Emmaline on the floor. "You must be very upset about this."

"Well, it is a bit upsetting, but Mr. Pickles is a sweetheart. I know he didn't spill the jar on purpose, did you Mr. Pickles?" said the Jeweler. She patted Mr. Pickles on the head.

"Yes. An accident. . . . Such a *tragic* accident," said Bagalon. "Nevertheless, you can't be happy about it, can you?"

"Well no, of course not," the Jeweler replied.

Bagalon leaned closer. "Maybe you would even say you are *un*happy?" Bagalon asked with a hint of suspicion in her voice.

"Well certainly. It will take me the better part of a day to clean up, even with your help Emmaline. And I'm afraid Mr. Pickles's tongue will never be the same."

"Well," said Bagalon, "I think I can help you."

"Really? You'll help me pick all these little metal flakes off the ground? You're so sweet, Bagalon."

Bagalon's lips squeezed together. Her head turned sideways as her eyebrows bent into a fold over her nose. "Goodness no! I was thinking of something else."

"Oh," said the Jeweler. She paused from picking up flecks of metal and looked around the workshop. "What did you have in mind, if you don't mind my asking?"

"We should go see the Queen. She'll tell you what to do," Bagalon replied.

The smallest of smirks, which the Jeweler mistook for a smile, appeared on the corners of Bagalon's mouth.

Helping the Jeweler

THE THREE WOMEN, Bagalon, Emmaline, and the Jeweler, stood before Queen Iliana. The Queen did not look well, her hair was messy, her eyes and shoulders drooped, her face was pale and she still wore the same nightgown from the previous three days. Her voice was raspy when she spoke, and if she spoke, it was a slow, painful process.

"Ladies," the Queen whispered as she nodded to the trio, "To what do I owe the pleasure?"

Before Emmaline had a chance to speak, Bagalon replied, "We're here regarding the Happiness Law, in particular as it relates to the Jeweler."

"The Happiness Law?" said the Jeweler. "I thought we were going to ask the Queen what to do about the spilled powder."

Bagalon stepped forward, in front of the Jeweler, and continued. "Your Highness, Emmaline and I were walking in town and heard a shout from the Jeweler's store, so we went inside and discovered the Jeweler's cat, Mr. Pickles, had knocked over a jar of powder. *Iridescent* powder. It made a terrible mess."

"And what of it, Bagalon? A little iridescent powder hardly seems worth talking about."

"My point, Your Highness, is the Jeweler was very *unhappy*." Bagalon rocked back on her heels and smiled the same, smug smile that she wore at the Jeweler's store.

"WHAT!?!" screamed Queen Iliana. She leaped out of her seat. "HOW COULD THIS HAPPEN? THIS IS A TRAGEDY!" She grasped the Jeweler's shoulders and stared into her eyes. "Is this true? Are you unhappy?"

"Well, I guess so. When Mr. Pickles jumped on the table—"

"Horrible! Tragic! Dreadful!" screamed the Queen. She spun in a circle and clutched her unkempt hair. "And in my kingdom too! Here you are, right in front of me, *unhappy*."

"I wouldn't say I'm unhappy. Well, maybe just a little. Really, it's not a big deal—"

Without pausing, Bagalon shouted, "GUILTY! That's what you are! Guilty! You are guilty of being unhappy! The nerve! How dare you disobey the law?"

"Well, I didn't really *do* anything," said the Jeweler. "See, it was Mr. Pickles, and I'm sure it was an accident. He's a very nice cat—"

"You are guilty of unhappiness! Don't try to blame this on your cat!" Bagalon pointed a finger at the Jeweler and poked her in the chest. Bagalon looked like she wanted to push her finger right through the Jeweler. The Jeweler, on the other hand, appeared confused and on the verge of crying.

"SILENCE!" shouted Queen Iliana, as she threw her hands in the air.

The Jeweler closed her mouth. Emmaline had never seen the Queen in such a tizzy.

Bagalon took a deep breath, smiled, and took a step back. "We can't allow people to break our laws whenever they want and expect to get away with it, can we, Queen Iliana? It would be chaos."

28

Emmaline raised her hand. "Your Highness, I don't think that this really is a problem. It's just a minor—"

"Oh be quiet, Emmaline!" said Bagalon. "You don't know anything about happiness and laws. You're just a little kid. The Jeweler broke the law, and therefore must be punished for committing a crime!" Bagalon crossed her arms over her chest, spread her feet wide, and stared at the Jeweler.

"Punished?" asked Emmaline. "Does she really need to be punished, Your Highness? Maybe we could just get Mr. Pickles a toy to play with, so he's less likely to knock over

another bottle. I bet that would make you happy, wouldn't it, Jeweler?"

The Jeweler nodded in agreement.

Queen Iliana appeared confused. She looked like she was trying to do the right thing but wasn't sure what it might be. She shook her head sideways twice, then said, "I sentence you to. . . . The punishment is . . . um . . . ," the Queen said. "I don't know what the punishment should be. We've never had this problem before."

"Well," said Bagalon. "Considering the Jeweler is a convicted felon, and we need to set an example to all the unhappy people in the kingdom, I would say a fine of three golden klonbeks would be appropriate. You should *insist* on it."

The Jeweler's eyes widened. Emmaline sucked in a breath of air and didn't let it out.

The Queen sat up quickly. Her eyes focused on the Jeweler. "Done! Jeweler! You are hereby fined three golden klonbeks for being criminally unhappy," said Queen Iliana.

"THREE GOLDEN KLONBEKS!" the Jeweler cried, having forgotten she was speaking to royalty. "It will take me *years* to earn three golden klonbeks! I can't possibly pay that! I'd have to sell my shop! And my tools!"

"You should have thought of that *before* you decided to become a criminal! If you can't pay the fine, then you'll have to be sent to the dungeon," said Bagalon.

Emmaline frowned. "Do we even have a dungeon?" she asked.

Bagalon threw her hands in the air. "It's a castle! Of course there is a dungeon! Isn't there, Your Highness?" The Queen nodded in agreement.

"But I didn't do anything! It was Mr. Pickles, and he's just a cat!"

"Tut, tut! Again trying to blame the cat. Away with you." Bagalon extended the fingers of her left hand as if to shoo away a fly. "Emmaline, escort the criminal to the dungeon and update the law to state anyone caught being unhappy will have to pay three golden klonbeks or be sent to the dungeon. Isn't that right, Your Highness?"

Queen Iliana blinked a few times, nodded, and said, "Yes. Yes of course, Bagalon. That is for the best."

Emmaline bit her bottom lip, curtsied, put her arm around the Jeweler's arm, and led the crying woman away. Queen Iliana flopped into a large chair, rubbed her temple, and moaned.

"Bagalon," she said, "I never knew this law would be so difficult. It's giving me quite a headache."

"Oh, there, there, Your Highness, don't be upset," Bagalon said. "You did the right thing. You can't have unhappiness running amok in the kingdom. If you're not careful, it will quickly turn to gloom, then gloom to despair, and despair to misery. It's best to nip this in the bud before a plague of misery falls on the kingdom. You are very wise to do what you did. Very wise. The Jeweler will thank you one day. Just wait and see. You don't need to worry about a thing."

"You're quite right. . . . We can't have unhappiness run amok."

"That's right, Your Highness. And with Queen Pixoratta's visit coming up, it is even more important, don't you think? You don't want Pixoratta to arrive to find a bunch of people with frowns on their faces, do you?"

"Absolutely not, Bagalon. Absolutely not." Queen Iliana coughed, then sat up a little bit, and pressed the tips of her fingers together. "I am so excited for their visit. Just think, Pixoratta, Queen of the Fluffles, is coming to visit with her entire entourage. I hear Fluffles are the sweetest, nicest, fuzziest creatures on the planet. I can't wait to finally meet them!" A coughing fit suddenly shook the Queen's body. When she was able to speak again, she grabbed Bagalon's hand in hers and looked deep into her eyes. "I'm sorry I haven't been feeling well lately. I wish I could do more with the party."

"Don't worry about anything, Your Highness. I will take care of everything."

"Thank you so much, Bagalon."

"I even sent riders to greet them on the road with welcome presents—some candy."

"Oh, Bagalon, what would I do without you?" Iliana patted Bagalon's hand and slumped back into the chair.

"Don't worry about a thing. Besides, before long everything will be mine." Bagalon's voice slid out of her mouth like a snake charmer as she bowed low before the Queen.

A question appeared on Queen Iliana's face. She furrowed her eyebrows. "I'm sorry, Bagalon. Did you say, 'Before long everything will be *mine*'?"

"Oh Heavens no! No! No! No! I said, 'Everything will be *fine*.'"

"Ah. I see," said the Queen.

But, unfortunately, for dear Queen Iliana, who only wanted the best for her country, she did not see. Not at all.

ATTENTION!

By order of Her Majesty Queen Iliana, it is hereby decreed that all residents, at all times, now and forthwith, for time eternal, be happy.

Or you will be fined three golden klonbeks and be sent to the dungeon.

The Queen's New Dilemma

BAGALON PATROLLED THE TOWN with Emmaline and found the Jeweler was not the only one having a hard time with the Queen's new law. . . .

Mr. Bluffmartin, an expert at bird calls, could mimic over seven hundred different calls by using his mouth, lips, hands, and a piece of driftwood. On Tuesday afternoon, while practicing the call of a cat-tailed-tiger-hawk—a most awful sound which involves blowing out one's mouth and sucking in through one's nose at the same time—Mr. Bluffmartin unfortunately snorted a passing wasp up his left nostril. "Bleugh!" he shrieked as he sneezed the wasp back out his nose.

Bagalon witnessed the entire ordeal and ran over.

"Are you happy about snorting a wasp up your nose?" she asked.

"Most definitely not!" he choked.

"GUILTY!" Bagalon cried.

Bella, a weightlifter and the strongest person in the town, was lifting a heavy barbell over her head on Wednesday morning when one of her chickens decided to chase a chipmunk. The chipmunk ran across the porch, through the front door, and into Bella's foot, where the chicken pecked it. Only *it* wasn't the chipmunk. *It* was Bella's toe, which the chicken had mistaken for a scampering chipmunk.

"Ow!" Bella cried.

The chipmunk scurried off, but Bella dropped the barbell right on top of her chicken. "Oh, no! My poor chicken!" She picked up the flattened bird and hugged it tightly to her chest.

"Are you sad you flattened your chicken?" asked Bagalon.

"Absolutely!"

"GUILTY!" Bagalon shouted as she pointed a finger in the air.

On Thursday, Davinda, a terrific trapeze artist, graceful gymnast, and astonishing acrobat, stood at the end of the town's diving board. Not the low one—the high one. Standing far above the pool, she looked like a small ant wearing a pink bathing suit and flowery swim cap. Davinda flexed her knees, leaped into the air, spun three times, and twisted twice before smacking the water like a whale dropped from a hot air balloon. Slowly, painfully, Davinda wiggled her hands and eased herself to the side of the pool. Her belly, legs, and arms were bright pink, brighter than even her swimsuit.

"Oh my heavens!" cried Emmaline. "Are you OK?"

"Oh. Ooh. Oh," huffed Davinda. "That really hurts."

"You must be very sad to have hit the water so hard," said Bagalon.

"Well, that was the first time I ever managed to do three flips, so I'm actually quite happy."

"Oh. But what about your towel?", said Bagalon.

"What about my towel?" Davinda asked.

"The wind just blew it into the pool."

"Aigh! My towel! Now I won't be able to dry off. How sad!"

"GUILTY!" yelled Bagalon.

Time and time again Bagalon shouted "GUILTY!" until everyone in the small kingdom had been caught being criminally unhappy, fined three golden klonbeks (which they of course couldn't pay), and sent to the dungeon.

It was a truly dark time for the kingdom.

But it was about to get even worse.

The Dungeon

THE DUNGEON IN THE CASTLE CONTAINED a single cell suitable for holding one person comfortably. Two people would have been able to play a game of cards on the floor and three people might have been able to have a tea party if everyone kept their elbows tucked in. Four people would have spent a large amount of time saying *excuse me, sorry for stepping on your foot*, and *do you mind moving your elbow? It's poking me in the back.* But put the entire town in one small cell? Impossible! And yet, that is exactly what happened. Townspeople were crammed into the small cage like stuffed cabbages.

After the Jeweler, Humungo the Blacksmith was thrown in. Not a small man, he took up a large portion of the back wall. Bella, the weightlifter, was the next to be tossed in. She leaned against a wall and had a pleasant conversation with Humungo about arm-wrestling, until the Baker and her husband arrived. Of the five, three were exceptionally large.

"I hope we're the last of them," the Blacksmith said. "There's not much room back here."

"Oof! There's not much room up here either," the Baker's Husband replied. His large belly pressed through the bars.

Then the small man with the round glasses was shoved into the cell. The guards squeezed him underneath the

Blacksmith's burly legs. Davinda appeared next. She tucked her body under Bella's arm, her right leg under the Baker's chin, her left arm around Humungo's back, her neck on the Jeweler's shoulder, and stood on one foot like a wrung-out heron. Next, Mr. Bluffmartin squeezed in around her and put his driftwood bird call into Bella's long hair since that was the only place it would fit.

"So sorry. I didn't mean to elbow you," he said.

"You didn't elbow me," said the Bella.

"I didn't?"

"No."

"Then who did I elbow?"

"I think that was me," said the Blacksmith.

"No, that was my shoulder," said Davinda.

"Is that your heel, Snookie-Bear?" the Baker asked her husband.

"No, it's my knee," said the small man with the round glasses.

More and more townspeople arrived and were pushed, prodded, and packed into the small cell. Arms stuck through the bars. Here, part of a face poked out. There, an elbow emerged from someone's hair. And over there, next to an ear, was a foot. It was impossible to tell where one body ended and another began.

"C'mon! Get in there!" cried Bagalon as she stuffed the last arm in the cell and squeezed the door shut with her shoulder, leaning on it with all her weight. She put a rusty key in the rusty lock and turned it, sealing the townspeople in the little cell. She pocketed the key and turned to Emmaline. "Let's go," Bagalon said. "Queen Iliana will want a full report."

"Wait!" cried the Jeweler. "When do we get out of here?"

"When you pay the three klonbek fine," Bagalon replied.

"But we can't work if we're in prison, and if we can't work we can't make money, and if we can't make money we can't pay the fine! Wait! Come back!"

But Bagalon didn't come back.

Later that night, Queen Iliana sat at her dining table as Bagalon gave a full report. "Well? Is everyone happy yet?" the Queen asked.

"We have successfully rounded up all the unhappy criminals and, just like you wished, have dealt with them," Bagalon reported.

"No one seems happy, though," added Emmaline.

"Of course they don't!" said Bagalon. "If they were happy, they wouldn't have committed a crime in the first place."

"I just think that if you want everyone to be happy, maybe there are other ways of going about it," Emmaline replied.

Bagalon put a hand to her chest and gasped. "Emmaline, are you suggesting Queen Iliana doesn't know how to best run the country? Queen Iliana is the smartest, wisest, most beloved queen in the entire world. She knows everything there is to know about happiness. Otherwise she wouldn't have told you to throw everyone in the dungeon," said Bagalon.

"*Everyone* is in the dungeon?" Queen Iliana asked. "You're telling me *every* single person—man, woman, and child—is currently locked in the dungeon, unwilling to pay the fine? Emmaline, is that true?" The Queen laced her fingers through her hair and pulled.

"Yes, Your Majesty," Emmaline replied.

"My goodness! What are we going to do? They were supposed to pay the fine and be happy again." She wrung her hands together.

Bagalon put an arm around Queen Iliana's shoulders. "Don't worry, Your Majesty. I'm sure they will change their minds. Just give them a few days in the dungeon. They'll come around. You just need to be patient."

"Yes. We'll just have to wait a bit for them to pay the fine, won't we?" Queen Iliana folded her arms across her chest and raised an eyebrow.

"Well, um, that might not work," said Emmaline. "You see, the, um, *criminals* don't have the money, and since they are in prison they can't earn any money, so I'm not really sure how they will ever be able to pay the fine. We—"

"Enough!" cried the Queen. "Oh, my head is killing me! I'm so confused. I can't take this anymore. Please leave me be. I need some time alone."

And so Bagalon and Emmaline stood up, excused themselves, and left Queen Iliana sitting alone in the empty dining room. The table was bare. No clinking sounds came from the kitchen. No delicious smells wafted from the oven. No servants stood at attention waiting to bring her food.

Through the headache and fog of confusion, Queen Iliana thought, *Where is my soup?*

Where is Everyone?

LATER THAT EVENING, Queen Iliana still sat at the dining room table. She had never gotten up because lunch had never been served, which was something Queen Iliana in her sickness could not comprehend. Every day, for her entire life, lunch had been served promptly at noon, and not being served at noon was so inconceivable that she simply sat at the table and waited. She waited for an hour, and then another. She was confused. Her head hurt. She coughed continually. Yet nothing happened. In the afternoon, no one served tea and biscuits, nor was dinner served that evening. Only when the sun began to set and long shadows fell across the empty table did Queen Iliana finally realize something was amiss.

"Emmaline!" she cried.

"Yes, Your Highness," Emmaline said as she scurried into the room.

"Where is my lunch? I haven't gotten my lunch yet."

"Well, Janelle is locked in the dungeon, so she couldn't make your lunch today."

"Oh. I see. Well, no matter. Just have Hervé bring me some milk and cookies," the Queen said.

"Um, Hervé is in the dungeon too."

"Fine! Then I'll go get some milk and cookies myself." The Queen's chair groaned as she pushed away from the table and turned towards the kitchen.

"Um, that's not possible either," said Emmaline.

"What do you mean? It's only a few steps to the kitchen. Don't you think I can walk a few steps?"

"No, it's not that," Emmaline stammered. "Farmer Francis is in the dungeon and he hasn't been able to milk the cows, so we don't have any milk. And the Baker is also in the dungeon, so no cookies either."

The Queen looked at Emmaline as if she had just seen a dancing hippopotamus perform a pirouette.

"I'm so confused, Emmaline. Are you telling me we have no cookies? No milk? No soup? *No food*?" the Queen asked.

"Yes, ma'am. With everyone in—"

"And we don't have anyone to milk the cows, collect eggs, or bake sweets?"

"That's correct. Everyone is in the dungeon."

"Everyone. I don't understand. How can everyone be unhappy? Ugh. Now I'm unhappy. And my headache is killing me. I think I should just go to bed and see if I feel better in the morning. We can let everyone out of the dungeon tomorrow. This new law is definitely not working. Have Lucinda turn my sheets down."

"Ma'am?"

"Yes, Emmaline? Please don't tell me you have more bad news."

"Um . . . Lucinda is in the dungeon as well. But that's probably OK since Hervé was thrown in jail before he could finish washing your bedsheets. They're still soaking in the washtub. I'm so sorry, Your Majesty. I bet if you let Hervé and Lucinda out of the dungeon—"

"I CAN'T TAKE IT ANYMORE!" the Queen screamed. "MY BRAIN IS GOING TO EXPLODE! THAT DOES IT! GET OUT OF HERE! I WILL DO EVERYTHING BY MYSELF!"

Emmaline scurried out of the room. Tears filled her eyes. She had never seen Queen Iliana act that way in the many years she had spent with her. Never, not even a single time, had Iliana ever yelled at Emmaline. The young girl ran down the hall and fled back to her quarters. Her tears kept her from seeing Bagalon in the hallway hiding behind the dining-room door. Bagalon snuck out from behind the door, rubbed her hands together as if she were warming them over a fire, grinned, and tiptoed down the hallway in the opposite direction.

Meanwhile, Queen Iliana skulked off to the royal laundry room. *Stupid, good-for-nothing cook,* she thought. *Can't even make a simple lunch before getting thrown in jail. And don't get me started on the lack of cookies and milk! Honestly! What were those people thinking, being unhappy? How hard is it to just be happy?*

She pulled the sopping sheets from the washbasin and twisted them between her hands. Dirty water and brown bubbles dripped down her arms. *Bleugh,* she thought as a murky puddle appeared around her feet. *How does Hervé do this every day?* She squeezed until no more drops of water dripped out from the linens then marched the soggy pile to her bedroom. Queen Iliana threw the clammy sheets on her bed and stretched them out into a swampy covering over her mattress. She flopped onto the sheets with a loud squish.

There! See, that was easy. Hervé's got nothing to be upset about, she thought. As she lay on the bed, cold water seeped through her dress, matted her hair, and chilled her skin. She felt as if she had lain down on a very large, very smelly, very wet sea sponge.

"Gaagh!" she screamed again. She pounded her fists into the soggy sheets. "This is the most uncomfortable bed ever! Forget it!" She rolled out of bed, walked across the room, and lay down on a large rug in front of the enormous fireplace in an effort to warm herself. Carved eagles adorned the mantel, which was made from blue and black marble and sculpted by the famous artist Glindernoot. Ornate fireplace tools stood at attention next to the fireplace. The only thing missing in the fireplace was an actual fire. As it so happened, the royal builder of fires had landed in the dungeon after getting a nasty (and very unhappy) splinter. Since then no fires had been made.

The Queen lay on the floor, shivered in her soggy dress, and tried to sleep through her confusion and headache. *Tomorrow, I will let everyone out*, she thought.

The Night Visitor

AT THE DARKEST PART OF THE NIGHT, when even the moon slept, a figure crept into Queen Iliana's bedroom. It wore a long dark dress, walked slowly, quietly, and carried a wooden staff. A cold voice whispered in the dark. "Iliana. Wake up, Iliana. It's time for your next treatment." The figure stumbled through the dark room to the bed. A loud thump was followed by the sound of the figure saying some rather unpleasant things about what the bed had done to her shin.

The room was still. Darkness seeped over the furniture.

Bagalon's voice murmured in the darkness.

"Boram ipsula flom bipsum."

As Bagalon finished saying the words, a faint red glow appeared above the bed and slowly brightened, illuminating Bagalon's face and hands in a reddish fog, but leaving her body invisible in the darkness. One hand held her staff, and at the end of the staff, where the gray stone normally was trapped by twisting vines, now a glowing red stone entwined in the carving, as if the stone itself had absorbed all the heat in the room and started to glow.

Bagalon waved the staff over the empty bed.

"Where are you, you old hag?" She spoke a few more words and the stone glowed more brightly. She walked around the room, poking the staff into corners, where the red stone lit up the edges of the room. "Ah, there you are!" The stone glowed above Queen Iliana, who slept in her soggy dress on the rug in front of the cold fireplace.

Bagalon bent down and shook Iliana by the shoulders.

"Wha? Bagalon? What time is it?"

"Flob smipsum bas fazzah!" she replied. The stone brightened and blazed with red swirls, spinning faster and faster, then turned to clear glass, a red whirlwind spiraling inside. Fiery storm clouds burned and smoke danced inside the glassy orb. Bolts of lightning leaped from cloud to cloud. It looked like a snow globe the devil would keep on his desk.

Queen Iliana's eyes stared into the swirling flame.

"Yes. That's right. Look into the flame. Look deep into the flame. It's very pretty, isn't it?"

"Very . . . pretty . . . ."

"It's a very pretty stone, isn't it?"

"Pretty . . . stone." Queen Iliana's face was still. Her eyes didn't blink. Her mouth hung open.

"You *insist* everyone in your kingdom is always happy, don't you?"

"Yes. . . . Everyone . . . happy . . . always."

"And you *insist* no one goes against your wishes."

"No . . . one."

The fire burned inside the stone and swirled like a trapped beast anxious to break free of the glass. Heat and smoke emanated from the stone.

"And Bagalon would never lie to you. You don't like it when people lie. You *insist* they tell the truth."

"Bagalon . . . never . . . lie."

Bagalon smiled. She spoke a few more words and the fire inside the orb at the end of the staff swirled into a tornado, spinning feverishly in circles. It got brighter and brighter until the entire room was filled with brilliant red light. A small sun blazed at the end of the staff and poured heat into the room. Smoke danced inside the stone, then outside the stone, then swam through the air like fiery eels until they finally crawled up the nose and mouth of the Queen. The Queen gasped and fell backward onto the rug, fast asleep.

Bagalon slumped forward.

The light in the orb faded. The stone turned gray. The room got very cold.

Checking on the Prisoners

THE FOLLOWING DAY, QUEEN ILIANA awoke in front of the cold fireplace with a terrible headache. She was drenched in sweat, even though the room was icy. She coughed several times before rolling over onto her hands and knees; her joints creaked as she pushed off the ground and stood halfway up; she groaned, then pushed on her lower back with one hand and rubbed her neck with the other; the right side of her hair looked like it had spent the night fighting the left side, and neither side had won. Her eyes were bleary and red and hid beneath puffy eyelids.

"Lucinda!" Queen Iliana doubled over in a fit of coughing. "Lucinda! Please bring me a change of clothes." Queen Iliana's scratchy voice echoed in empty hallways. Lucinda did not answer. Lucinda, as you might remember, was locked in the dungeon with everyone else.

"Darn it, Lucinda," the Queen said to herself. "Janelle! I need some tea, just a little bit for my throat. Where are you, Janelle?" Janelle did not answer either, as she was also locked in the dungeon's small cell, squished somewhere between Lucinda, Hervé, and Mr. Bluffmartin.

"Is no one around?" the Queen said to the walls.

No one answered.

Queen Iliana changed out of her wet clothes, put on a wrinkled dress, and dragged her feet down the hallway towards the great room, where she hoped she would find a fire and hot tea. Instead, she found Bagalon sleeping in a large chair. The Queen flopped down in the chair next to her. Bagalon blinked then sat up.

"My goodness, Bagalon! How long will these criminals hold out? They're destroying the kingdom!"

"I have no idea, Your Highness. They do seem very stubborn."

"I need to get rid of the law. It's not working. It's time we let everyone out of the dungeon."

"What? No! No. I mean. . . . Don't do that. They'll come around soon. Don't get rid of the law."

"Yes. We need to get rid of the law. It's causing more trouble than it's worth."

"Are you sure—" Bagalon started, but the Queen had already begun down the hallway towards the dungeon. Bagalon ran after her. "These are hardened criminals, Your Highness! Every last one has served time! Don't go into the dungeon! It's not safe for you to be around them. Let me talk with them. It would be bedlam to release so many unhappy people all at once, Your Highness. Utter chaos!" The Queen continued striding towards the dungeon. Bagalon raced to keep up with her. Once they reached the cell, Bagalon squeezed her body between Queen Iliana and the prisoners. She leaned in close to Iliana and whispered, "Let me talk to them, just to be safe. These are dangerous prisoners and you're the Queen. I would hate for anything to happen to you."

Queen Iliana stopped and looked at the wall. She squeezed her eyes together and nodded. She took a step backward and waved Bagalon forward.

Bagalon stood in front of the prison cell and looked at the sleeping bodies inside. "You there!" she said as she poked an elbow sticking out between the bars. "Wake up! Farmer Francis! Why aren't you looking at me?"

"That's my elbow," said Lucinda's sleepy voice from two faces over. "His elbow is over there."

"Ah." Bagalon poked another elbow.

"Good morning, Bagalon," Hervé said from somewhere in the mass of bodies.

"Yes. Good Morning, wherever you are," Bagalon replied. She took two steps over and patted Farmer Francis on the cheek. "Now, tell me, why is it you're unhappy? What landed you in the dungeon? Why can't you follow the law and be a good citizen? Hmm? Tell me."

"Ah, well, you see, everything was wonderful until Celine was thrown in the dungeon."

"And why is that?" Bagalon asked.

"Well, Celine played her flute every night to let the cows know it was time to come home for the evening milking. Without Celine's music, my cows never came home. I still don't know where they are and I can't go look for them because I'm locked in a dungeon, which is making me even more unhappy."

"I see. . . . And you do realize being unhappy is what landed you in the dungeon to begin with?"

"Well, yes, I suppose so."

"Well then, until you become happy, it seems you're going to be spending a lot of time in the dungeon." Bagalon crossed her arms and scowled at Farmer Francis.

"I'm happy! Can I come out?" yelled a voice from the bottom of the pile of prisoners.

"I'm happy! Let me out," cried another person.

"Me too!" shouted Mr. Bluffmartin.

Bagalon frowned.

"I'm happier than anyone!" said the small man with the round glasses.

"No, I'm the happiest! Let me out!" yelled Bella.

Suddenly, there was such a clamor of townspeople claiming to be happy that it sounded like Great Flubnuk's Eve at the colosseum. The Queen smiled and clapped her hands together. "Oh Bagalon, isn't this wonderful! Everyone is happy!"

Bagalon grabbed Queen Iliana by the shoulder and pulled her away from the cell bars. Then she whispered two of the worst words ever whispered in history. Words that would prove to be so awful, I cringe to mention them here and can only hope you skip over the next paragraph to save yourself the horror of reading them.

"They're lying."

Bagalon's voice was calm. Her lips curled up at the sides as she said those fateful words.

"What's that, Bagalon? I can't hear you. Everyone's yelling and smiling," said Queen Iliana.

"They're lying." The worst words ever whispered, twice in one day.

Queen Iliana glanced through the cell bars. "What? Look at them, Bagalon. They all look perfectly happy to me."

"Impossible. First, they're criminals," Bagalon said as she counted off on her fingers. "Second, they didn't pay the three klonbek fine. Third, they are squished in a dungeon like worms between a Zibnet's toes. There is no possible way they could be happy. They *must* be lying."

"Why. . . . Well . . ." said the Queen. "I had never thought about that. You there! Baker! Are you telling me the truth? Are you *truly happy* locked up in my dungeon?"

"No, ma'am," the Baker replied. She hung her head. "I'm sorry I lied to you, but I'm miserable in here."

"Well what about you, Jeweler? Are you telling me the truth?"

"No, Your Majesty. I was hoping if I told you I was happy you'd let me out. I'm sorry."

"Good gracious! Is everyone lying to me?"

A chorus of contrite *Yes ma'ams* and *I didn't mean to's* and *please don't be mad at me's* came from inside the cell.

"See! I told you they were lying," whispered Bagalon.

"Well! I am beside myself with anger! Shame on you! Shame on every one of you! Not only are you criminals, but you also lied to me! Didn't your parents teach you to never lie? How dare you! What has this world come to? Bagalon! I'm feeling faint! Ooh . . . my head!"

"Shh. . . . There, there, you poor dear," Bagalon muttered as she held the Queen in her arms. She turned and led Queen Iliana away from the prison cell. "Everything will be fine soon. You just need some rest. I told you visiting with criminals might be too dangerous for your health."

"Oh, Bagalon! You were right! I can't go on! Being Queen is so hard! You have no idea."

"You just need a little peace and quiet, Your Majesty. A little rest and you'll be as good as new in no time. A vacation. Come with me. I know a perfect place for you to get some time away."

"Yes. . . . A little rest. . . . Some time away . . ." the Queen muttered.

A Permanent Vacation

QUEEN ILIANA WALKED IN A DAZE down the hallway, leaving the townspeople squished in the prison cell behind her. Bagalon reassured her that everything would be fine soon. Very soon. The two walked down a second hallway, turned down a third, and then a fourth. Queen Iliana started to feel like a mouse in a maze with no cheese. Bagalon stopped the Queen and snuck a glance back the way they'd come.

"OK. Good. There's no one here to see us," she said.

"How is that good?" the Queen asked.

"Um. . . . So no one can interrupt your . . . uh . . . vacation," replied Bagalon.

"A vacation?"

The two snuck down the hallway. Bagalon put a small key into a tiny hole in a side wall and opened a secret door. She crouched down and snuck through the doorway.

"I never realized there was a secret door down here," said the Queen.

"There are a lot of secrets you don't know about," muttered Bagalon.

Bagalon led the Queen down a dark, twisty passageway that smelled like rotting mushrooms. The darkness was overwhelming. They slid their hands along wet, mossy walls in order to make their way forward. A minute later, the Queen caught the slightest whiff of fresh air. Soon, the hallway brightened; light streamed through an opening at the far end of the tunnel; they continued forward and stepped out onto a rock ledge jutting out from the side of Mount Gazooka, the largest and most massive mountain in the kingdom. A narrow path, barely wide enough for a single person to stand on, clung to the side of the mountain.

"This way, Your Majesty." Bagalon took the Queen by the hand and pushed her out onto the ledge. Rocks skittered beneath the Queen's feet and tumbled down the cliff wall.

"Bagalon, I can't go out there!" the Queen huffed. "I'm scared of heights, my head hurts, my legs feel like jelly, and I'm so *confused*. Why would they lie to me?"

"Just a little bit more," Bagalon replied.

"I really think I—"

"No, keep going!" Bagalon pushed Queen Iliana forward up the narrow path. Then more softly, "There's a nice place just a little farther up the mountain. It's the perfect spot for a vacation."

Queen Iliana dragged her feet along the trail. Her legs buckled underneath her as she held a hand out against the cliff wall. Bagalon grabbed the Queen and pushed her forward to a small outcropping high on the face of the mountain. There, a cave opened into the mountainside, while an ominous rock—larger than the cave opening itself—sat next to it.

"We're here," Bagalon said as she pushed Queen Iliana into the cave. "This will be a wonderful vacation spot. No one will bother you here, or be unhappy, or lie to you."

"Oh, thank you so much, Bagalon! You are a dear, dear friend. What would I ever do without you?"

"You're too kind, Your Highness."

"Don't be silly. . . . You've taken care of everything. You thought of the happiness law. You arrested all those unhappy criminals. You fined them and you threw them in the dungeon; you caught them lying, and you even snuck me out of the castle without anyone seeing just so I could have a vacation. I'm just so exhausted and confused. My head hurts. My brain doesn't seem to be working. You don't have any idea how much I appreciate everything you've done."

"You're very welcome, Your Majesty." Bagalon bowed low before the Queen. "Come with me. Let me show you a special throne I had built just for your vacation."

They walked into the cave. Dusty rocks littered the cave floor. In the far corner sat a massive stone chair carved from a single piece of solid rock. Other than the throne, the cave was entirely empty.

"Thank you so much, Bagalon. Is that the throne? My! It looks dreadfully uncomfortable."

Bagalon took Queen Iliana's hand. "Here you are, Iliana. Sit down on your vacation throne and relax."

"Oh Bagalon, it *is* dreadfully uncomfortable. Who would make a chair out of a rock? I shouldn't take a vacation. I should go back to the castle. This is a bad idea."

"No!" Bagalon yelled, then, more gently, "I mean, no, you stay right where you are. I'll bring you a comfy pillow, something soft. Here, suck on this candy. It will soothe your nerves. She pulled an exceptionally large pink candy out of her pocket and pushed it into Queen Iliana's mouth.

"Mmmf!" said Queen Iliana.

"It's OK, Your Highness. It's good for you. It will help you relax. You need a vacation to gain your strength before the Fluffles arrive." Bagalon massaged Iliana's cheeks. "Pixoratta and her entourage won't be here for another few days. I have everything under control. You just relax."

"Mmmf! I tofally forgomf the Flufflef!" Queen Iliana started to stand up but Bagalon put a hand on her shoulder and pushed her back down.

"Go to sleep if you want. Oh, but before you do, could you just sign this?" Bagalon pulled a piece of parchment out of her pocket.

"Whaf if thaf?" asked the Queen through the candy. She stifled a yawn.

"Oh, it just says you're going on vacation and will be back soon, but if anything should come up that needs to be dealt with, like planning the party, you'd like me to deal with it for you. Just so you won't have your vacation interrupted. You can't be too careful, you know."

"Oh Bagalon, you are fo fweet. You have foughf of everything! I just need a quick naaa," the Queen replied. She stretched and yawned.

"Yes, a nap. But sign this paper first, so you won't be interrupted later. There you go. Right there at the bottom. Just stay awake until you finish signing it. . . . Perfect! What a big yawn, Your Majesty. You just go to sleep. . . . Sleep. . . . Sleep. . . ."

The queen's head lolled forward.

Bagalon backed out of the cave and rolled up the piece of paper containing the Queen's sleepy signature.

"Sleep. . . . Sleeep. . . . Sleeeeeeep. . . ," she continued. At the mouth of the cave, Bagalon whispered, "I'm just going to close the door so the light doesn't come in and wake you. You just sit and sleeeeeeep. . . ."

"Mmmm . . ." the Queen murmured.

Bagalon snuck behind the unusually large rock at the cave's mouth. Jammed underneath and hidden behind the rock was a rope tied to a lever. Bagalon reached into a hidden pocket in her dress. She wrapped her hand around the bloodwood handle of a sharp dagger. A twisting dragon's neck adorned the side of the blade. Bagalon flicked her wrist. The knife flashed and cut the rope in two, freeing the lever. The enormous boulder rolled towards the cave opening, *thunked* loudly, and sealed Queen Iliana inside. Her vacation throne quickly became a soundproof crypt.

Bagalon danced and shuffled her feet and threw her hands in the air and laughed and shouted. "I did it! I actually did it! Ha ha! Good riddance, Your Dumminess! Have a nice vacation, Queen Stupid! Ha ha ha! Enjoy your nap, you old hag! It's the last one you'll ever have!"

She slid the knife with the twisting dragon's head carved into the bloodwood handle back into the secret pocket in her dress and climbed down the mountain.

The Nun of Gligoonsburg

IT WAS NIGHTTIME. Bagalon sat at the writing desk in Queen Iliana's bedroom and examined her handiwork. Happy with the outcome, Bagalon rolled the parchment closed and tied it with a red ribbon. She lit a candle, dripped hot wax on the paper, and pressed the seal—the Queen's official seal—into the wax. She let the wax cool, placed the document on the Queen's desk, and, after checking the hallway both ways, snuck out of the Queen's bedroom. She scurried back to her own chambers, slipped under the bed covers, and pretended to sleep.

Bagalon didn't have to wait long, as Emmaline soon walked down the hallway and rapped her knuckles on the Queen's bedroom door.

"Your Highness? Are you awake?"

Bagalon bit her pillow and snickered under the sheets. There was no answer from inside the room, so Emmaline tried again, and again was met with silence.

Bagalon pushed the pillow from her face and threw the covers on the floor as she leapt out of bed. She ran to her bedroom door and straightened her dress. The smile left her face and was replaced with a bored look, as if nothing interesting had happened in the past few hours or months or years. She opened her bedroom door and stepped into the hallway.

"Emmaline, how are you this morning?" she said in a boring voice.

"Not very well, Bagalon," said Emmaline. "I can't find Queen Iliana anywhere. Have you seen her?"

Bagalon's face quickly changed to one of concern. "No. Is she not in her bedroom?"

Emmaline tested the door, which was unlocked. She pushed the door open a crack and peered in. She saw the Queen's bed, still sopping wet from the dirty linens. The Queen's nightgown, also wet, lay in front of the cold fireplace. But there was no sign of the Queen.

"She's not here," said Emmaline.

"That's odd. What about that document on her desk?" asked Bagalon. "Perhaps that's a clue. Who is it addressed to?"

Emmaline looked at the rolled-up parchment and read the name on the outside. "Why! It's addressed to me."

"Yes. Yes, it is. There's your name right there. You should open it."

Emmaline slid a finger under the wax seal, unrolled the document, and read:

I, Queen Iliana, decided to sail to Gligoonsburg to become a nun. Don't follow me. Bagalon is the new queen. You have to do everything she says.

Ilia

"Oh my heavens!" Emmaline cried out.

"What shocking news!" feigned Bagalon. "Whatever will we do? I couldn't possibly be queen." She put her hand to her chest and took a deep breath.

"But it looks like you'll have to. The Queen has commanded it." Emmaline examined the letter. "This is so astounding. And odd. Look—the Queen's signature seems different, like she fell asleep while writing it. Look how her name trails off. That's not her normal signature. And it's not her handwriting either."

"It looks like the Queen's handwriting to me. Perhaps she was just in a hurry when she wrote it," said Bagalon. "It is definitely the Queen's signature, so that makes it an official document."

"I guess so. And it was sealed with the Queen's official seal," said Emmaline. She tapped her fingers on the desk and chewed the corner of her bottom lip. "Oh! I'm sorry, Bagalon!" Emmaline suddenly bowed down on one knee and lowered her gaze. "All hail Queen Bagalon!"

"Oh please, Emmaline!" Bagalon blushed, hiding a smile behind the back of her hand. "We're friends here! Just call me Your Excellency."

The New Queen

THE NEXT DAY, after being released from the dungeon, hundreds of townspeople assembled in the courtyard below the castle's main balcony. It was where Queen Iliana had thrown white roses every year to celebrate the beginning of winter. On this day, however, Bagalon stood in the middle of the balcony, Emmaline stood shyly to her side, and Queen Iliana was nowhere to be found. Bagalon waved her hand for silence and addressed the crowd.

"I know you are all very excited to be out of the dungeon—"

The crowd cheered and clapped and hooted and hollered uncontrollably. Someone screamed, "We love you, Bagalon!" Another voice shouted, "You're the best, Bagalon!"

"Quiet down. Quiet down. I couldn't bear the thought of you being in that dungeon and just had to let you out." More cheering.

"Please settle down. Settle down. I have a very important announcement. You may be wondering why Queen Iliana is not here to make the announcement herself. Well, it is because Queen Iliana has left and is no longer with us." A murmur ran through the crowd. Bagalon reached back and pulled Emmaline to the front of the balcony. "Emmaline will read the official statement."

Emmaline's hands trembled as she unrolled the forged letter. Beads of sweat ran down her back. She took a deep breath and read, "I, Queen Iliana, have decided to sail to Gligoonsburg and become a nun. Don't follow me. Bagalon is the new queen. You have to do everything she says. Signed, Queen Iliana."

The townspeople stopped shouting. Some rubbed their heads. One swooned.

"Astonishing!" said Davinda.

"Extraordinary!" cried the Baker.

"Unprecedented!" said the small man with the round glasses.

"Gligoonsburg? Where's Gligoonsburg?" said Humungo.

A quiet fell over the crowd. No one spoke. No one coughed. No one knew what to do. Confusion flowed between the townspeople like a muddy river.

"Ladies and Gentlemen," Emmaline said, her voice wavering, "Queen Bagalon!"

She waved a hand at Bagalon. The townspeople bent down on one knee before their new queen. They bowed their heads and Bagalon, er, excuse me, *Queen Bagalon*, stepped forward.

She had somehow changed clothes and now wore a lavish, purple-violet flowing dress with gold and diamonds sewn into the seams. The fabric twinkled like a million fireflies. A golden crown shimmered above her head, giving the impression the sun had decided to follow her. She waved at the people below.

A chorus of "Long live the Queen!" rose from the streets.

"Please! Please! Thank you! Oh, you're too kind! Thank you! Thank you so much!" Bagalon waved a hand to quiet the crowd. "Phew! So much excitement! I see you are all as excited as I am. And I bet you have a lot of questions for your new Queen. Well, let me say I am completely devoted to you, my loyal subjects! So, the very first announcement is I'm getting rid of that horrible law old Queen What's-Her-Name made about having to be happy all the time. From now on, I declare that no one has to be happy ever!"

The crowd screamed and shouted.

"Hooray!" yelled the Baker's Husband.

"Yay!" cried the Jeweler. "I've never been so happy to be allowed to be miserable!"

"I can't wait for something awful to happen so I can be sad about it!" said the small man with the round glasses.

Queen Bagalon once again waved for silence. "In addition, no one has to pay the three golden klonbek fine!"

More cheers.

"And lastly, no one will *ever* be put back in that awful, stinky, damp, dark dungeon!"

The crowd erupted in deafening applause.

Over the next few days, Queen Bagalon (forgive me, for I still have a hard time referring to that dreadful woman as *Queen*) began ruling the kingdom. She went from house to house assuring the townspeople she would be a fair and just queen. She would make certain her subjects were happy and well taken care of. She would be the best possible queen ever.

The townspeople wondered about Iliana and her sudden desire to become a nun as they enjoyed their new freedom.

Everything was wonderful.

Until, a few days later, when the Fluffles arrived and everything changed.

Baking with Fluffles

"Hee hee . . ."

A tiny voice.

"Hee hee hee . . ."

Another tiny voice.

"Did you hear that?" the Baker asked her husband. She stopped kneading dough on her wooden workbench, cocked her head to the side, and listened. The Baker's Husband froze. A half-eaten donut stuck out of his mouth.

"Hee hee . . ."

"There it is again!"

"I dimf hear nyfning," he said through the jelly donut.

"Shh!" she replied.

"Hee—"

"There! Over there! It's a Fluffle!"

Sure enough, in the corner, hiding behind an open cabinet door, was a fuzzy brown creature. It was perhaps a head or two shorter than the Baker, putting its yellow eyes at the height of the wooden countertops. Its hairy toes stuck out from underneath a fat furry belly. Yellow toenails poked out like moldy hooks from its feet. Short, furry arms stuck out from its sides like broken pine branches, and, at the end of one, a grubby hands clasped a metal pitchfork. The creature's pointy teeth glistened as drool dripped from ghastly lips.

"Aigh! Get that nasty thing out of my kitchen!" screamed the Baker.

The Baker's Husband grabbed a cookie sheet and swung. *BAM!* He smacked the cabinet door. *BLAM!* The cookie sheet crashed onto the floor. *SWACK* against the leg of the workbench. As each mighty swing came, the Fluffle skipped out of the way, leaving a trail of drool behind. It leapt onto the counter and hopped over the Baker's huge bowl of flour. *SMASH!* The Baker's Husband sent the bowl flying through the air. A white flour snowstorm filled the room. The Fluffle's drool mixed with the flour to form gray clumps as it danced about the room.

"Hee hee hee! You can't catch me!" it screeched and foamed.

The Baker grabbed a large metal frying and swung it at the creature's head, but the Fluffle gently leapt off the counter, slid between the Baker's Husband's legs, and poked him in the rear end with the pitchfork.

"OUCH!"

A second Fluffle crawled out from the pantry and snuck up behind the Baker. It was a nasty creature, even more greasy and more drooly than the first. It too held a large pitchfork, which it poked into the Baker's rear end just as she was about to flatten the first Fluffle.

"Hey! That hurt!" she cried.

The two Fluffles scurried out of reach. They leapt and bounded about, scattering pots and pans and spices all over the kitchen.

"Don't be a dork and sit on a fork," one of the dreadful creatures sang.

"Don't be grouchy. It's just a little ouchie!" sang the other.

"I'm not a dork! And I didn't sit on a fork, you idiot! You poked me!" shouted the Baker's Husband.

"He seems grouchy," said the first Fluffle.

"Of course I'm grouchy! You poked me in the butt with a pitchfork!"

"Hee hee hee!" the two Fluffles giggled as they jumped and licked the wooden spoons with their gray-green tongues.

"Aigh!" screamed the Baker. "I can't take any more of these dreadful creatures! They're ruining my kitchen! They're ruining my bakery! They're ruining the kingdom!"

From behind the Baker, a voice dripped. In the doorway stood Queen Bagalon. Her black dress poured down around her shoulders.

"Ruining the entire kingdom? Really? My my! That is a rather grandiose claim," Bagalon said.

The Baker spun to argue with the stranger in the doorway, then froze as she eyed Bagalon.

"Queen Bagalon! Your Highness!" she squawked. "I had no idea you were here."

"Indeed you didn't," Bagalon replied.

The two Fluffles jumped off the counters, raced behind Queen Bagalon and, like small children, hid behind her dress, clutching the fabric with their nasty yellow claws and holding on tightly.

"There, there. I'm sure the Baker didn't mean to scare you, my little darlings," Bagalon said to the Fluffles. She patted each on the head, flattening their greasy fur. The Fluffles smiled sharp yellow teeth.

"It's impossible to get anything done with them around," said the Baker.

Bagalon held up her hand. "Please," she said, "dear Baker, if you don't like to keep a tidy kitchen, that is your business. But we must be nice to our guests."

"Yes, Your Highness," the Baker sighed. Peering out from behind Queen Bagalon, one Fluffle squished his lips together, pushed his eyebrows down, put a single claw inside each nostril, and turned his nose up, displaying the contents of the inside of his nose to the Baker and her husband.

"At any rate," Queen Bagalon continued, "is everything ready for tonight's party? It must be a smashing success."

"Yes," the Baker sighed, "everything is ready, or it will be by the time the party starts."

Queen Bagalon looked around at the splintered cabinets, the broken pots, the flour scattered everywhere. "Yes, well I believe you can handle the 'smashing' part, but can you handle the 'success' part? Never mind. Don't answer that. Dweezil! Weezil! Come with me."

The two Fluffles hopped out from behind Queen Bagalon. Dweezil stuck out a tongue and *phththted* at the Baker. Weezil did the same to the Baker's Husband. Then the two furry fiends slapped their hands together, shook their butts, and followed Queen Bagalon towards the castle.

"If I never see either of those creatures again, it would make me a very happy person," said the Baker.

More Fluffle-Trouble

The Sunken Anvil

AS QUEEN BAGALON WALKED down the cobblestones of the town's main street, Fluffles appeared behind every corner, inside every doorway, and through every window. Four Fluffles raced out of the blacksmith's shop, carrying Humungo's large anvil over their heads. The Blacksmith raced after them.

"Get back here with my anvil, you miserable creatures!" Humungo shouted.

"Hee hee hee!" they giggled.

"I mean it! I'll smack you with my blacksmith's hammer! I'll turn you into horseshoes!" he yelled.

"Oooh! That ugly giant is so scary . . . ," sang the first Fluffle.

"His arms are big and hairy . . . ," sang the next.

"We'll really have to avoid his wrath . . . ," sang the third.

"Once we give his anvil a bath!" yelled all four in unison. They heaved the heavy anvil high into the air. Up, up, up it flew. It spun slowly as it sailed over the short wall around the town well. Down, down, down into the well it fell. *Kasploosh!* Water erupted from the well and dripped off the Fluffles' greasy fur as they ran away in four different directions. Humungo looked over the edge of the well and watched the ripples on the water slowly fade.

"Now what am I going to do?" he cried.

Queen Bagalon walked past. "Tut-tut," she said. "Such a shame your anvil fell in the well. You really must take better care of your tools."

"Those dang Fluffles threw my anvil in the well! They should be punished! Make them go get my anvil!"

"Firstly, Blacksmith," said Bagalon as she poked a finger into his chest, "I am the Queen, and no one tells me what to do. Especially not a blacksmith. Secondly, the Fluffles are our guests. You need to be nice to them."

"But they threw my anvil in the well!"

"Blacksmith! I'd hate for them to hear you. Maybe in their kingdom throwing anvils is a sign of great respect."

Humungo rolled his eyes.

"At any rate," Queen Bagalon continued, "we're having a party tonight and I must have a pony ride for our guests. We'll have the fifty smallest ponies in the kingdom and they will all need new horseshoes, so you better get working on those right away."

"But my anvil is at the bottom of the well . . . ," said Humungo.

Barbells and Fruit Salad

Farther down the street, a loud clang rang out. Three Fluffles ran out of Bella's back door, two ran out her front door, and one leapt through a side window, landed in a rosebush, greasily slid between the thorns, and raced off.

"Get out of here, you miserable creatures!" the bodybuilder screamed. She threw a barbell at the fleeing Fluffles.

"My goodness!" said the small man with the round glasses. "What happened?"

"It's those Fluffles!" she cried. "They changed all the numbers on my barbells, so now I don't know how much each one weighs. The heavy ones are light and the light ones are heavy."

"What's so bad about that?" asked the small man with the round glasses.

"Look at my arms! My muscles are different sizes! This arm is huge while this arm is tiny."

Bella flexed. Sure enough, one bicep was gigantic and the other was much smaller, although it was still much bigger than either of his.

"Now when I do pushups, pullups, overhead curls, renegade rows, or goblet squats, I get all crooked and twisted because my muscles are different sizes."

"Oh my!" said the small man with the round glasses. "I never knew bodybuilding demanded such precision."

"Yes. Now I've got to go work out just my left arm for an extra hour, but I don't know which weights to use."

She sighed as she watched the Fluffles disappear down the road.

"I'm sorry," she said. "I don't mean to burden you with my problems. I suppose they've been bothering you too?"

"Oh heavens yes!" the small man with the round glasses replied. "Just yesterday they came into my office, poured apple sauce on my chair, jammed a banana in my pencil sharpener, squashed cherries on the raffle cards, and threw a rotten cantaloupe at the picture of my grandmother."

"Ooh! That's horrible!"

"It looked like a fruit salad exploded in my office. I still haven't finished cleaning it up. But the worst was the stupid song. I can't get it out of my head.

Hee hee hee!
Hoo hoo hoo!
Fruit salad is good for you!
Don't be sad.
Don't be glum.
Have yourself a rotten plum!

"And then they shot a plum across the room with a slingshot. It hit me right in the face!"

"That's *dreadful*," said Bella.

"What are we going to do?"

Queen Bagalon silently appeared behind the two townspeople. "I'll tell you what you're going to do," she said. "You're going to get ready for tonight's party. Isn't that wonderful? Bella, tonight you'll finally set that world record. I'm sure of it."

"Do I have to?" The bodybuilder seemed particularly unexcited about trying to set any record, world or otherwise.

"Of course you do. Our *national pride* is at stake. We must have the world record for the most number of bricks one person can stack above her head in one hand."

Queen Bagalon turned and looked at the small man with the round glasses. "And you have the raffle cards for the party. They're ready, aren't they?"

"Well, not really," he replied. "You see, some Fluffles came into my office and squashed cherries in the cards, so they're ruined."

"Oh, you're such a kidder! Ruined! I doubt it. Next time just make sure you spend less time making fruit salad and more time making raffle cards," said Queen Bagalon.

"I didn't make any fruit salad! The Fluffles came into my office and—"

"Yes, I already heard all about it. Dweezil and Weezil told me how nice you were to invite them for lunch. I wish everyone would show them the same hospitality."

"I didn't invite them! They snuck in my office and started throwing food," the small man with the round glasses said. "There was no hospitality."

Bella snarled as she punched a clenched fist into an empty hand. "How 'bout if I show them our famous *hospital*," she said.

"No. No. No," said Queen Bagalon. "You misheard me. I said *hospitality*. Not *hospital*. Very different. You should start doing ear exercises so you can hear better. Ha ha ha ha!" Queen Bagalon wiped away a tear. "See you tonight! Don't forget—raffle cards and a world record. Nothing less!"

The Shattered Chandelier

Queen Bagalon passed in front of the Jeweler's house. The sound of metal crashing on wood rang out. A Fluffle scurried out the front door.

"Oh no!" cried the Jeweler from inside her house. "I am not happy about this!"

"That's fine," said Bagalon. "Now that I'm the queen, you're allowed to be unhappy. Isn't that wonderful?"

"Oh, Your Highness," said the Jeweler. "That Fluffle just ruined the chandelier I've been decorating for tonight's party. I just finished polishing it when that creature jumped up on my workbench and threw the chandelier across the room. Then it threw every bottle of paint I own across the room as well."

"Please, Jeweler. If I recall correctly, Mr. Pickles did the same thing once."

"Mr. Pickles knocked over *one* bottle, and it was an accident. That Fluffle broke my chandelier on purpose! Look at that nasty creature—it's laughing at me!"

"Well, that's because Fluffles are naturally happy."

"They're naturally *rotten*, is what they are," said the Jeweler.

"Tut-tut," said Queen Bagalon. "You mustn't speak of our guests that way." The Queen put her arm around the Jeweler's shoulders. "Don't worry about the broken chandelier. I'm sure it's no big deal."

"Really, Your Highness? You don't mind that it's broken?"

"Heavens no! It's just a chandelier. The important thing is no one got hurt."

"Oh, thank you so much! I thought you'd be upset there wouldn't be a chandelier for tonight's party."

"Of course there will be a chandelier."

"You told me not to worry about it."

"Absolutely. Don't worry about the broken one. You just worry about making a new one," said Queen Bagalon.

"But it took me three weeks to make the first one!"

"Like I said, just worry about making a new one. Besides, the party doesn't start until seven o'clock. It's noon now, so that gives you a few hours."

"I can't—"

"Oh, but you must, Jeweler! I have the utmost faith in you! I'll see you and your new chandelier tonight!" Queen Bagalon smiled and walked away. The Jeweler stood on her porch. Large tears welled up in her eyes.

As Queen Bagalon walked back to her castle, more and more townspeople appeared on their front steps and porches. Davinda held a bathing suit with holes cut out of it. Mr. Bluffmartin puffed on a broken bird call. The Fluffles had secretly replaced Lucinda's shampoo with glue and her deodorant with a stick of butter, so her hair stuck out in every direction and her armpits smelled like sweaty toast. They nailed Janelle's bed to the ceiling. They poured honey on Celine's hats. Bees surrounded the poor girl whenever she went outside.

The party was only a few short hours away, yet the entire town wanted nothing to do with it, Queen Bagalon, or those dreadful Fluffles.

The Fluffle Party

THAT EVENING, THE TOWNSFOLK DRESSED in their finest clothes. They combed their hair. They shined their dancing shoes and met in the castle's Great Hall.

Humungo was there. He had managed rescue his anvil from the well and craft two hundred new horseshoes for the Queen's tiny ponies. He should have been proud of his accomplishment, but instead was upset. The way the Fluffles were racing the ponies around the dining table, he would need to make a few replacement horseshoes before the night was through.

The Jeweler was there. She stood on a tall ladder and hooked the new chandelier's chain to a fastener in the ceiling. She hadn't had time to make the chain as strong as she'd wanted, but it would do.

Bella was there. She was arranging bricks in the corner to be used later for her attempt at setting the completely useless brick-stacking world record.

The small man with the round glasses was there. He stood in front of the ballroom doors and handed out inky raffle cards which turned the guests' fingers blue.

The Baker and her husband were there. She put the finishing touches on a grand seven-layer cake. Frosted with white icing, filled with buttercream, drizzled with chocolate, it had a small figurine of Pixoratta, Queen of the Fluffles, at

the very top. But if you looked closely, you'd see the figurine was not made of chocolate, as was the Baker's usual choice, but instead from some black licorice found on the pantry floor behind a can of olives.

Emmaline was there as well. She had spent the afternoon making sure everything was in order—dishes, plates, and flowers on the tables, drinking glasses, and so forth. She checked again as Queen Bagalon barked orders at her about how the silverware was crooked and the napkins were folded incorrectly.

And of course, Queen Bagalon was there in all her splendor. Her hair sparkled with jewels—thousands of tiny diamonds and sapphires adorned her head. They caught the light from the chandelier, sculpted it, and sent it dancing around the room. She flitted from guest to guest and Fluffle to Fluffle before clinking a knife on her wine glass.

"Ladies and Gentlemen! It is a great honor to have you join me in this evening's grand festivities!" A faint clapping arose then quickly faded from the room.

"And," the Queen continued, "it is even more of an honor, indeed an absolute delight, for me to welcome our guest of honor this evening, the beautiful, the charming, the oh-so-sweet leader of the Fluffles, Queen Pixoratta!"

Queen Bagalon raised her wine glass even higher and waved it towards the ugliest, greasiest, yellow-toe-nail-iest, slobbering-iest, and most disgusting Fluffle ever seen, Queen Pixoratta. Wax dripped from her ears like melting cheese. Yellow-green mucus slid from her nose and squished on the floor between her rotting toenails. Her greasy fur appeared to have been coated from crawling through a sewer pipe, but you wouldn't want to get close enough to find out. Her fingernails—claws really—were three times longer than any other Fluffle's, three times more yellow, three times more crumbly, and eighteen times more smelly. It was, and excuse me for saying so, nearly impossible to look at Pixoratta, Queen of the Fluffles, without having a sudden and overwhelming urge to throw up.

The Fluffles jumped about. They popped in and out of curtains and raced ponies down the length of the dining room table. They appeared behind doors, on top of hats, and under evening gowns. They shouted and cheered for their disgusting queen.

The townspeople, on the other hand, were much less enthusiastic. There were a few faint-hearted claps from time to time, as well as some small *yays*, but not much else.

"Ladies and Gentle—Ack! Haak! Haaaaak! Phleugh!" Queen Pixoratta of the Fluffles coughed up a gob of green goo and spit it onto the white tablecloth. Bits of phlegm clung to nearby glasses and silverware.

"Ladies and Gentlemen, thank you so much for welcoming us into your arms and hearts as your guests. You are wonderful hosts. It's so delightful to be here." Queen Pixoratta bent her greasy head towards the crowd. As she bent over, she lifted her left foot, scraped out a piece of chewing gum from between her toenails and popped it in her mouth.

"And we," Queen Bagalon said, "love having

you here with us. To the Fluffles!" She brought her wineglass up to her mouth, took a sip, then threw the rest—wineglass and all—over her shoulder. The crystal smashed into the stone wall and splintered into thousands of razor-sharp raindrops. "Please, sit, enjoy the meal, and let the merriment begin!"

The Fluffles hooted with glee and bounced about the room in excitement.

The guests took their places at the enormous dining table. A townsperson sat next to a Fluffle who sat next to another townsperson who sat next to a Fluffle and so on around the table, such that each townsperson was surrounded by two Fluffles and each Fluffle had the choice of two townspeople to pester during the meal.

Waiters dressed in their finest suits placed baskets of warm rolls and butter on the table, which the Fluffles grabbed in their yellow claws, bit off chunks, and spat across the table at each other. Gobs of butter and half-eaten slobs of sticky yellow goo stuck in fur and fancy dresses. Then the waiters brought plates with a lovely mixed-green salad which the Fluffles also threw across the room. Bits of carrots stuck in Davinda's hair. A juicy tomato slid down Humungo's forehead. Normally, one might expect to see a nice appetizer, perhaps cheese and crackers, but that night, by special request of Queen Bagalon, the wait staff served squid tentacles—slimy, gooey, *mucilaginous*, squid tentacles. (*Mucilaginous*, in case you didn't know, is a big word to describe the goo behind a slug as it crawls across a sidewalk.) Fluffles grabbed tentacles and snapped them at each other like wet towels. The suckers slid harmlessly off their greasy fur, but stuck, quite strongly, to the townspeople's exposed skin, which was particularly bad for the small man with the round glasses and his bald head. Two Fluffles, one on each side, braced their feet on his shoulders, grabbed the stuck tentacles, leaned back, and pulled as hard as they could. Slowly, painfully, the suckers *pop, pop, popped* as they unstuck from the poor man's head. The small man with the round glasses was soon covered with not only bits of salad and butter, but also hundreds of tiny red welts.

Each new course of food provided fresh ammunition for the Fluffles. Creamed chicken, broccoli with cheese sauce, linguini, applesauce and mashed potatoes flew across the room. A bright red beet stew rained down on the townspeople. Nothing was off limits to the Fluffles' furry fingers.

As the meal came to an end, Queen Bagalon clinked a knife on the side of her second wine glass. "Ladies and Gentlemen," she said, "one more course awaits. Dessert! Our very own Baker has made a most wonderful cake. Look at all those layers of frosting. My, that looks good! But before we get to that, I have an exciting announcement."

Macaroni and cheese dripped from the walls and splatted on the ground.

"Tonight, Bella will break the world record for stacking the most number of bricks over her head at one time!"

A piece of lettuce slid down the Baker's Husband's face. Gravy dribbled underneath Lucinda's shirt and down her back.

The townspeople cheered and, for the first time of the evening, were happy to be at the party. The Fluffles too. They jumped and hooted and sang their dreadful songs.

"Bella, please begin! Stack those bricks! While you set that record, we will cleanse our palates," said Queen Bagalon. "Emmaline, be a dear and serve the candy."

Bella stood up and wiped the salad, applesauce, gravy, and bread crumbs from her evening gown. She walked over to the large stack of bricks waiting for her in the center of the room. She grabbed a wide board, balanced it in her powerful right hand, bent over, picked up a brick, and placed it on the board. She picked up two more bricks and placed them on the board. A small pyramid began to form.

Emmaline walked into the kitchen and brought out a bowl of small green candies. The Fluffles, who had been distracted with behaving horribly, raced at Emmaline. Pixoratta leapt at the bowl of candy, crashed into it, and sent hundreds of green candies flying through the air.

Pandemonium broke out amongst the Fluffles.

"CANDY! CANDY! CANDY!" they cried.

Fluffles leapt into the air. Their yellow fingernails shot out like hungry frog tongues catching flies. Their teeth gnashed. They pushed and poked and kicked each other. They scrambled over, under, and through townspeople to get at the green candies. From above, it looked like a feeding frenzy at a greasy, furry, fish pond.

In the center of the room, Bella continued to stack bricks.

At the head of the table, Queen Bagalon was pleased. "My, they certainly do enjoy cleansing their palates, don't they, Pixoratta?"

Pixoratta, Queen of the Fluffles, didn't answer. She didn't hear a word Queen Bagalon said. Pixoratta was caught up in the excitement. "CANDY! CANDY! CANDY!" she screamed. She jumped over her subjects and stuffed as much of the green candy in her mouth as she could. "Gimme that! Mine! Mine! Mine!"

Emmaline stood still, her mouth half open, and watched the Fluffle Queen leap about.

In the furor, a small piece of candy skittered across the table unnoticed by the Fluffles. Davinda picked up the candy between her fingers and placed it in her mouth. Her eyebrows came together. She made an odd face, as if she had just sucked on the wrong side of a lemon.

Bella continued to stack bricks in the center of the room. By now, the board held a very large pile. Her arm muscles twitched. The stack, although not record-setting, was much larger than any other person in the town could have possibly held in one hand, except for maybe Humungo. It had grown much too high for her to reach the top, so instead, she bent down, grabbed a brick, tossed it up into the air, and caught it on the top of the pyramid.

"Oooh! Well done, Bella!" exclaimed Queen Bagalon. She clapped her hands with excitement. "Only a few more to go and you'll have the record!"

Davinda shrieked. She spit the slimy green lump on the table. "That's disgusting! It's the most awful candy I have ever tasted. Baker, how could you make that?" She took the only clean corner of her napkin and furiously scrubbed green residue from her tongue.

The Baker, horrified, replied, "I didn't make that. Those are from Queen Bagalon's secret recipe."

Davinda's spit-out piece of candy caught the attention of three nearby Fluffles. They cried in unison, "CANDY! CANDY! CANDY!" Each jumped at the slimy green chunk. They scrambled over each other. They tore out tufts of fur and bit each other's legs. A foot kicked the tiny piece, skidding it across the table, where it lodged between Pixoratta's toes. Pixoratta looked down, saw the green lump, and quickly stuffed all four toes into her mouth. She sucked the piece of candy from between her yellow toenails. She closed her eyes. A smile of pure bliss settled on her face.

"Oooh! Everyone look! Bella only has three more bricks to go to set the record!" cried Queen Bagalon. "Quiet now! Quiet everyone! She needs her concentration."

The townspeople watched Bella.

The three Fluffles had seen the candy slide under Pixoratta's foot, the foot which was now stuck in her mouth. They dove across the table at her. "CANDY! CANDY! CANDY!" they cried.

Emmaline jumped to the side to get out of their way.

Bella bent down and picked up the second-to-last brick.

The small man with the round glasses said, "Ooh! This is so exciting, don't you think?"

"Very!" the Baker's Husband agreed.

Pixoratta opened her eyes, which immediately widened at the sight of the three candy-crazed Fluffles charging at her.

Bella tossed the second-to-last brick high into the air.

"Shh!" Queen Bagalon said to the small man with the round glasses. "Don't break her concentration."

The brick floated in the air.

Pixoratta gasped and sucked the candy into her windpipe, where it got hopelessly stuck.

A bead of sweat dripped down Bella's forehead. Her arm shook under the massive pile of bricks.

The three Fluffles crashed into Pixoratta and sent her flying off the table.

The next-to-last brick flipped in the air one last time before landing perfectly at the top of the pyramid of bricks, which almost reached the ceiling.

Davinda continued to rub her tongue. Her napkin turned green.

Bella struggled under the weight of the bricks. She said, "Only one more—"

Pixoratta hit the ground with one foot in her mouth. The other foot landed on the shards of Queen Bagalon's broken wine glass. "YEOW!" she cried, sending the piece of candy flying from her mouth.

"—brick to go. . . ," said Bella. She picked up the final brick.

The Jeweler clapped her hands with excitement.

Queen Bagalon said, "Well done—"

The three charging Fluffles bounced off of Pixoratta's empty chair and crashed to the floor.

The piece of candy flew from Pixoratta's mouth and popped one of the small ponies in the rear end. The pony bucked, sending the Fluffle riding it as well as a loose horseshoe through the air. The horseshoe sailed up towards the chandelier, and, with a quick crash, broke the chain holding it. The chandelier fell and landed right on top of Bella's precariously balanced brick pyramid.

The chandelier swayed forward.

The large stack of bricks swayed backward.

"What's happening?" said Bella. She looked up at the stack of bricks, now with a large chandelier resting on top of them.

"Careful!" cried Humungo.

The chandelier swayed backward.

The large stack of bricks swayed forward.

"It's too heavy! I can't hold it!" said Bella.

The pyramid of bricks swayed forward. The chandelier leaned over from the pile like the crest of a wave about to break.

Everyone—townspeople, Fluffles, and Queen Bagalon—silently stared at the swaying mass.

"Watch out! Take cover! It's going to fall!" Emmaline cried.

The Fluffles leapt from the table. They scrambled under chairs and raced under the table. (They were Fluffles, after all, and if Fluffles are anything, it is quick).

The townspeople, on the other hand, were not so fast.

The tower of bricks fell forward. Down the entire length of the table bricks rained from the sky. They shattered plates and bowls and wine glasses. They landed on the heads and ears and backs of the townspeople. They bounced next to Fluffles hiding under the table. The chandelier sailed over the entire table, spun in the air twice, and smashed into the seven-layer cake between Pixoratta and Queen Bagalon.

The cake exploded. Bits of frosting flew in every direction, covering Queen Bagalon in sticky delicious goo. Icing went in her hair. Cake got in her ears. The black licorice figurine of Pixoratta shot halfway up Queen Bagalon's right nostril.

"GAACK!" Queen Bagalon cried as she yanked the figurine out of her nose. She looked at the cakey mess on her dress, the shattered chandelier, the broken bricks, and the splintered chairs. "Emmaline! How dare you!"

(It is here I have to pause. If you are a smart reader, which I'm sure you are, you would not blame Emmaline for any of this disaster. You might blame the piece of candy that shot out of Pixoratta's mouth, or the loose horseshoe. Or you might blame the hastily built chandelier. Or the broken wineglass Pixoratta stepped on. Or, more likely, you might blame those dreadful Fluffles with their atrocious table manners. And you'd be right, and, at each turn, you'd realize the blame could be traced squarely back to Queen Bagalon herself, and not back to Emmaline, who had actually warned everyone to take cover.)

Emmaline's mouth was open, but no words came out.

"Well, I never!" exclaimed Queen Bagalon. "Honestly Emmaline! We have guests in our kingdom—delightful, charming guests—and *this* is the way you behave!"

"But I didn't do anything!" said Emmaline, quite correctly.

"You throw bricks at them! You smash their cake? I am so . . . so . . . *disappointed* in you! You are an embarrassment to the kingdom."

Queen Bagalon wiped cake from her dress and threw it at Emmaline.

"An embarrassment, I tell you! This is the worst night ever! Clean this mess up, Emmaline! And I mean everything! I don't want to see a single piece of lettuce, a bit of broccoli, a drop of beet soup, or a broken brick anywhere when I get back! Anywhere! Come on, Fluffles. I am so sorry you had to see that. Look at you, you poor things. You're shaking you're so traumatized by her bad behavior. Let Queen Bagalon make you feel better. Let's go to the royal swimming pool and get cleaned up."

The small man with the round glasses stood next to a table by the door. "What about the raffle? Aren't we going to do the raffle?"

Queen Bagalon stopped and looked at the table holding the stack of raffle cards.

"Here's what I think of your silly cards!" She swatted the stack and sent the wet cards flying. Queen Bagalon stormed out of the room. The Fluffles followed her.

The hall was quiet, except for the broken chandelier chain, which squeaked as it swung from the ceiling.

~ Intermission ~

Let me guess. You're thinking, *An intermission? I don't need a stinking intermission! I just did all that reading! I read about Queen Bagalon's rule and about the infestation of Fluffles in the kingdom. About the wonderful news that everyone was allowed to be miserable again. You shouldn't even have an intermission in a book! Who's the ding-a-ling who wrote this thing, anyway?*

Well, let me answer that question for you. My name is JJ McGeester and I'm the ding-a-ling who wrote the book, and if I want to have an intermission, I'm going to have an intermission. Maybe I want to go get some popcorn. Or perhaps I need to go to the bathroom. I'm sure I must have my reasons, and I don't have to share those reasons with you.

But if I did, it would be to tell you that very quickly the situation in the kingdom got worse and worse. Queen Bagalon was not, as she claimed, a warm and caring ruler. Not in the least. The townspeople's lives went from lovely, to good, to fine, to not-so-great but still OK, to bad, to rotten, to outright miserable. As the months passed, their faces sunk and their skin turned pale.

The Fluffles, led by Queen Pixoratta with evil Dweezil and dreadful Weezil, became so awful that if you talked about them, your mother would wash your mouth out with soap—horse soap, not that nice hand soap—and you'd sneeze bubbles for a week. The Fluffles' fur got greasier. Their fingernails turned even more yellow. Their breath smelled even more vile. They carried pitchforks wherever they went and were absolutely dreadful to the townspeople.

I would tell you that Emmaline, dear sweet Emmaline, was the very saddest, most miserable person ever to live. Queen Bagalon despised the young girl. Anytime anything went wrong, it was Emmaline's fault. Anytime anything needed cleaning (which was quite often with Fluffles around), Emmaline had to clean it. If it needed mending or scrubbing or flossing or clipping, Emmaline mended or scrubbed or flossed or clipped. Queen Bagalon locked Emmaline in a small room at night. You couldn't call it a bedroom since there was neither a bed nor much room.

You're thinking, *Oh, I know this story. This is the same story as Cinderella, who is miserable but she has a fairy godmother, and some nice mice who are really good at sewing, and a wobbly shoe, and some mean stepsisters, and a prince who likes wobbly-shoed, mouse-clothed princesses, and they all live happily ever after.*

And you'd be right. Except for the part about the fairy godmother and the nice mice who are really good at sewing and the wobbly shoe and the mean stepsisters and the prince and *especially* about living happily ever after. But, the part about Emmaline being miserable, well, on that item, you'd be correct.

So, if I were to explain to you why there is an intermission in the book, it would be so I could get on my ostrich and ride away. Far, far away. I would go away and cry. Because when I think of the kingdom, of that horrible Queen Bagalon, of the dreadful Fluffles, the desperate townspeople, and dear Emmaline miserably wasting away, well, it would be more than I could bear.

Which is why I won't explain to you why there's an intermission.

Two years later . . .

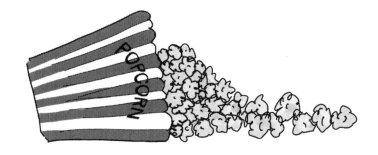

Sofia

EMMALINE LOOKED AT HER CHAPPED HANDS, red fingers, and cracked skin. She leaned her back against the damp stone wall and slowly slid to the floor. She looked around the room and saw three items—a ratty mattress, a torn blanket, and a small bucket. A single window with bars across it let a trace of moonlight into the dark room. She covered her face with her hands and cried. Large tears streamed down, leaving wet, dirty streaks on her cheeks, before splashing onto her dress.

"Why won't anyone listen to me?" she said to no one.

A rustling sound, faint and faraway, answered her.

Emmaline looked up and sniffled. She wiped the back of her hand along the bottom of her nose.

"Hello? Is someone there?"

From a dark corner, a pair of furry feet with short white claws crept forward. They clicked on the stone floor, then stopped.

"Come on out," said Emmaline softly. "I won't hurt you."

The feet inched forward. Attached to the feet were two skinny legs which quickly vanished into a furry body. The creature crept closer, stopping just shy of the puddle of moonlight on the floor.

"It's OK," said Emmaline. She wiped the other side of her nose.

The creature hesitated, then took two steps forward and stepped into the moonlight. It was not tall, and perhaps would have stood slightly higher than Emmaline's waist if the two stood next to each other. Small arms with furry hands and fingers stuck out from its sides; small, brown eyes, peered out from behind a mat of fluffy, dusty fur.

"Are you . . ." Emmaline paused. "Are you a Fluffle?"

The creature nodded, ever so slightly, and stared at Emmaline.

"You're smaller than the other Fluffles," she said. "And your eyes aren't yellow. I thought all Fluffles had yellow eyes. And yellow claws, too."

The small Fluffle looked at Emmaline. Its white eyes blinked.

"Are you cold? You're shaking. I can't imagine you'd be cold with all that fur. Do you want my blanket?"

Emmaline held out the scrap of fabric. Her fingers poked through the smaller holes.

The creature shook its head.

Emmaline put the blanket back on the ground.

"You sure are quiet. Can you speak?" Emmaline asked.

The Fluffle did not say anything. It stared at Emmaline. Its fur shook and shivered.

"Hmmm. . . . I guess not. What's your name?"

The Fluffle didn't answer.

"Oh, right. You can't speak. That was a silly question. My name is Emmaline and I—"

"Sofia."

"I'm sorry. What did you say?" Emmaline asked.

"Sofia." The Fluffle's voice was no louder than a falling piece of paper. "My name. It's Sofia," the creature said.

"Sofia. What a pretty name."

If it was possible to see behind the fur covering her face, you would have seen Sofia blush.

"How did you get in my room—" Emmaline started to say, but stopped. Sofia's fur suddenly stood on end. Her eyes widened. She stopped shaking and turned her small head towards the locked door.

"What? What is it?" Emmaline asked. She looked at the door and then back at the frozen Fluffle in front of her. "I didn't hear anything. . . ."

Emmaline turned back to the door and listened intently. She held her breath so as not to make a sound. Just as her lungs started to burn and she was about to breathe again, Emmaline heard muffled voices and the scratchy footsteps of two Fluffles walking down the hallway.

"Oh, it sounds like Dwee—"

She stopped. The space where the small Fluffle named Sofia had been was empty. Moonlight fell uninterrupted to the stone floor. A set of keys jangled in the door's lock.

"Where . . . where did you go?" Emmaline asked the empty room. The door banged open. Light from the hallway filled the room. Dweezil and Weezil, both holding pitchforks, burst in. Their yellow eyes peered at Emmaline. Dweezil put his face up against hers. His breath, from the bottom of a swamp, bubbled up and burned her nostrils.

"Where did *who* go?" he asked.

"What? Oh, no one." Emmaline replied. "I was just . . . um . . . talking to myself."

"Get on your feet, you stinky sausage!" Weezil poked Emmaline with a pitchfork. "Time to get to work!"

"But the sun hasn't even come up yet."

"Shuddup, brat! Move it!"

Weezil prodded Emmaline a second time and pushed her out of the room.

Dweezil followed, put one hand on the door to close it, then stopped. He turned back to the room, looked around a few times, and furrowed his eyebrows. He sniffed, three quick sniffs—like a bloodhound or wolf—and held the air in his lungs. His eyes squinted. He slowly let the air back out. He turned, walked out of the room, and closed the door behind him. The room got very dark.

Deep from within the darkness, high in the wall near the ceiling, two small eyes blinked.

The Duke of Dunglewood

QUEEN BAGALON SAT IN HER THRONE—Queen Iliana's old throne—contemplating what to do with Emmaline. *The castle is supposed to be clean, and yet,* she ran a finger across the curves of the armrest and inspected the small circle of dust as if it were an ink stain on the end of her finger, *Emmaline can't even do that. I really don't know why I bother with her.*

A guard entered the room, walked over to the throne, and whispered in the Queen's ear.

"Really?" she said. "The Duke of Dunglewood? Here? Already?"

The guard nodded.

"My! My! Yes, do send him in!"

Queen Bagalon stood up. She smoothed the folds of her dress, adjusted her crown, and sat back down. She shifted in her seat, crossed her ankles and tipped her head back in a regal—but not too haughty—angle. She examined the reflection of her teeth in the silver goblet on the table next to her.

"Your Majesty, the Duke of Dunglewood!" said the guard. He opened the large wooden doors at the entrance to the throne room. Framed beneath the doorway stood the Duke of Dunglewood. His shiny black boots and shiny black mustache matched his eyes. His black leather gloves wrapped tightly around his long fingers, making them look like snakes clutching the hilt of his sword. His black hair shone in the sunlight, while two large front teeth looked like they were trying to escape from under his upper lip. He paused to admire his reflection in a mirror before entering.

"Queen Bagalon!" he shouted. "You are absolutely beautiful! Ravishing!" He strode to the throne, bent down on one knee, and took her hand in his. "Stunning!" He kissed the back of her hand. "A masterpiece!" Another kiss. "A work of art!" And another wet, sloppy *smack* on the back of her hand.

"Oh, you're too kind," said Queen Bagalon.

"Never has my presence been blessed with a more heavenly creature. I fear I will go blind," the Duke said. He clutched his chest with one hand, put the back of his other hand on his forehead, leaned back, and teetered on his knees.

"Oh, you're such a charmer," Queen Bagalon replied.

"So," the Duke whispered, "I see our little plan worked. You fooled everyone with that note, even Queen Iliana. How did you do it?"

"Do what?"

"How did you kill her? I need to know." The Duke grinned and rubbed his hands together. "Did you slit her throat? Or maybe hit her in the head with a rolling pin? Or, oh! I know! Poison! Maybe put a drop or two in her wine, she takes a little sip, and *aaack!* No more queen!" The Duke clutched his throat and fell to the floor.

"No, I didn't slit any throats or bash any heads with rolling pins. You know me. I could never kill anyone," Queen Bagalon replied as the corners of her mouth started to grin.

"Did you tie a rock around her feet and throw her off a bridge? Or, better yet, feed her to the Swamps of Smugnuk? Down she goes, *blub, blub, blub*, until only her head is above the goo and then, *slurp!* Gone forever! Oh, I've always wanted to do that!"

"No, I didn't throw her off a bridge or into a swamp."

"Well then how did you do it?" The Duke stood up and placed both hands on his hips. "Stop keeping me in suspense!"

"I gave her a sleeping pill and sealed her in a cave. A big, huge, sleeping pill. She'll never wake up with that thing. And I rolled a big rock over the cave entrance and left her in there all alone. Isn't that precious?" Bagalon put a hand over her mouth and giggled.

"Oh, that *is* good. I've killed a lot of people, but never like that," said the Duke. He smiled and twisted his mustache between his fingers.

"Duke! I could never *kill* anyone! I couldn't hurt a flea. You know me! If she just happens to die in there, well, that's her fault. Oh, and even better, I told her she was going in the cave for vacation."

"No!"

"Yes! And, get this, I said I'd come back to get her. Ha ha ha! She believed me!" Bagalon laughed.

"Oh, that is so repugnant, I love it!" The Duke clutched his side. "You are an evil, nasty, wicked creature! I love you!" He took Queen Bagalon's hand and kissed it again. "There's nothing I like more than a woman who's not afraid to get what she wants. Marry me!"

"What? Marry you? Don't be silly!" Queen Bagalon pulled her hand back, but the Duke refused to let go.

"Think of it," he pleaded. "We're perfect for each other. Marry me! We can rule as king and queen. With your evil planning and my—"

"That's *quite* enough!" With her free hand, Bagalon grabbed the wooden staff resting against the throne and whacked the Duke of Dunglewood on top of the head. "I'm entirely capable of ruling without the help of some nitwit king, thank you very much. And, as I recall, none of your wives live very long after the wedding." She smacked him a second time.

"Ow! Ow! My head! You said you couldn't even hurt a flea!" he cried. The duke released his fingers and rubbed the top of his head.

"Oh, you poor baby." She patted his hand. "However, I *could* use a little more of your help. I have another job for you."

The Duke of Dunglewood looked up, interested. "I was wondering why you called me. Tell me more. Who is it this time?"

"You know Pixoratta, the Queen of the Fluffles?" The Duke nodded. "Well, she's. . . . Hmm. . . . How shall we say it? A *distraction*. Yes. She's become a distraction to me. The Fluffles obey her, and, as long as she obeys me, everything is fine. But she's starting to get her own ideas. It's time for her to disappear."

"You mean *disappear* like Queen Iliana disappeared?" the Duke asked.

"Yes. Exactly. I need Pixoratta to disappear. Forever."

"And by *forever*, you mean—"

"I want to never see her grubby little face again, you imbecile! Drown her in the Swamps of Smugnuk, stab her, throw her from the Cliffs of Nomor if you want. I don't really care. Do you think you can manage that?"

"Hmm. . . . I think I can manage something," the Duke smiled. He looked sideways and stroked his black goatee with a leather hand. "Maybe," he added.

"*Maybe*? Just maybe?" Queen Bagalon asked.

"Well . . ."

"Well what?"

"What's in it for me?" the Duke asked. "Surely having Pixoratta disappear forever is worth something."

"What do you want?"

"Well, since you refuse to marry me, maybe you could find me a wife? Someone to cook and clean for me. To wash my socks and clip my toenails. Clean the wax out of my ears. Massage my feet after a day of hunting. That sort of stuff."

"In other words, a slave."

"A wife, a slave, what's the difference? But, yes, a wife would be a lovely payment for my services," the Duke said.

The Queen rubbed her chin. She peered in the Duke's eyes.

"I think I know just the person," Queen Bagalon said with a twisting smile.

"Perfect! I'll make Pixoratta disappear by Saturday and we can have a wedding on Sunday at noon."

"Sunday at noon?"

"Sunday at noon," the Duke replied.

"You won't be late?"

"I'm never late for one of my weddings, although, I can't say the same for my wives." His left eyebrow twitched and the corners of his mouth stretched wider. "I do have quite a few *late* wives." He laughed at his very poor attempt at humor.

"It's a deal. You make Pixoratta disappear and we'll celebrate with a wedding on Sunday."

"At noon?"

"Precisely at noon."

"Excellent. I'll have my wedding tuxedo sent from Dunglewood." The Duke thought for a moment more before adding, "I do hope there isn't too much blood on it."

Emmaline Sees Sofia, Again

DWEEZIL THREW EMMALINE TO THE FLOOR of her bedroom. He looked around—slowly, as if he were looking to find a hidden spider or snake eggs. He put a toe under Emmaline's mattress and kicked it over, exposing the stone floor beneath. He snorted, walked out of the room, and slammed the door behind him.

Emmaline heard the familiar *click* as the deadbolt sealed her in.

She lay on the floor, unable to cry. Her eyes were closed. She rubbed the red welts on her arm where Dweezil's claws had torn her skin. Her hair fell over her face and the cold floor pressed against her forehead. *Just make it stop*, she thought. *Just make it stop. Just make it stop.* The phrase churned through her mind over and over and over. *Just make it stop.*

Long after Dweezil had left, a fingernail—a small, white claw—reached out from the darkness and brushed a lock of hair from Emmaline's face. She lay still, not caring who or what was in the room with her. The fingernail reached out a second time and gently pushed Emmaline's hair from her eyes. Soft, furry fingers wiped the tears from her face. Emmaline opened her eyes and saw Sofia's brown eyes looking back at her.

She sniffed and the brown eyes skitted away. They cowered in a corner of the room. Emmaline wiped her nose and propped up against the wall.

"I'm sorry I scared you, Sofia," she said. "I just . . . ." She paused. "Thank you."

Sofia turned her head and watched Emmaline from across the room.

Emmaline continued. "You're the only one who has been nice to me, so thank you." She lowered her head and gazed at the folds of her dress. She picked at a loose thread.

Sofia watched, then took a step across the room and then another. Slowly, the small Fluffle made her way over to Emmaline. She held out a small hand and lightly brushed Emmaline's arm. Her fur tickled Emmaline's skin. The edges of Emmaline's mouth turned up in a brief smile then sank back. Sofia bent down and nuzzled her body beneath Emmaline's arm, then she squeezed up tight. Sofia's soft, warm fur pillowed Emmaline's face.

"It's going to be OK, Emmaline. I promise," said Sofia.

The Duke Makes
Pixoratta Disappear . . .

THE NEXT NIGHT, the Duke of Dunglewood snuck around the outside of the castle, although you would have been hard-pressed to see him. His long, black coat, black pants, and even his black mustache were mere shadows in the darkness. The black sack, tied over his right shoulder, disappeared into the night. He moved like a puma, quickly, silently, and with purpose. The Duke slid, like ink spilling across a floor, to the rock wall underneath Pixoratta's window. And then the Duke disappeared.

Or at least, he seemed to disappear.

If your vision were better—maybe as good as a hawk's or eagle's—you might have seen the Duke leap from the ground, grab a small nick in the rock, launch his body up the wall, grab the next small outcropping, pull himself up, kick off a ledge, seize hold of a thin vine growing from the side of the castle and flip himself onto the ledge of Pixoratta's bedroom window, where he sat like a black cat, unmoving. But the Duke moved so quickly and so quietly, that to you and me both, it seemed that at one moment he was on the ground and the next he was crouching outside her bedroom window.

That wasn't so hard, he thought.

Peering into Pixoratta's bedroom, he saw the Queen of the Fluffles asleep in a small bed in the center of the room. Underneath the bedroom door, a light shone in from the hallway and cast the shadows of four clawed feet, the Queen's personal guards, waiting outside. The Duke slid into the room and drifted to the Queen's bed like velvet smoke. His black shape loomed over her small body. He untied the sack from his shoulder and held it in both hands.

From the hallway, he heard a noise, and froze in his tracks. He saw the shadows of the guards' feet move across the floor.

"So, everything's quiet?" said a voice from the hallway.

"As quiet as a mouse," a voice answered.

"Excellent. Pass me the candy."

"Hey! Don't hog it all!"

The Duke heard scuffling from behind the door, and then the voices trailed off and two sets of shadows walked away.

He looked back at the sleeping Fluffle queen lying on the bed in front of him. Green drool dripped from her mouth and stained her pillow. Her fur was slick with grease. Her yellow toenails had torn the bottom of her bedsheets to shreds. She breathed in, snorted, and breathed out. Her breath stunk like cheese growing between a giant's toes.

"Ugh!" the Duke whispered. He reached down with one hand and grabbed the Queen. He raised an arm to throw her in the black sack, but his black leather glove slid off her greasy fur. He tried again, but she slipped through his fingers, making his glove even more greasy. Queen Pixoratta grunted and rolled over. The Duke set the sack on the floor, opened the bag wide, and with both hands tried to lift Queen Pixoratta off the bed. She slid through his arms like a wet worm. Grease and small clumps of fur clung to the Duke's black gloves. He picked up the sack and pulled it over her head. Queen Pixoratta slowly sunk into the sack. The Duke inched it down to her feet, but as he did, one of the Queen's long toenails pierced the side of the bag. The Duke pulled out a long, black knife, and, with a quick flick of his wrist, cut the toenail right off her foot.

"Wha—" she yawned.

The Duke yanked the bag shut and quickly tied it closed.

"What are you doing? Hey! Let me out of here!" Pixoratta shouted from inside the bag. She squirmed and shook.

The Duke punched the bag with his fist.

The bag stopped squirming.

"Is everything OK in there, Queen Pixoratta?" came a voice from the hallway.

The Duke froze. He looked around the room, saw nothing of use, and answered in a high squeaky voice, "Everything's fine. I'm just having a dream! Ooooh! I'm flying!"

"Are you sure?"

"Yes! Ooh, now I'm falling, falling, falling. . . ."

"Weezil! Open the door. Something doesn't sound right."

The Duke heard the rattling of keys in the doorknob and then he disappeared.

Or at least, he seemed to disappear.

If your vision were better—maybe as good as a crow's or buzzard's—you might have seen the Duke of Dunglewood jump to the bedroom window, leap to the small crack in the side of the castle wall, try to grab on but instead leave a big, oily smear down the wall where his greasy glove slid, unable to clutch onto the ledge. You would have seen him tumble across the wall, crash into the turret and fall twenty feet to the ground. He would have looked nothing like a puma in the night—more like a dazed skunk—but only if your vision were as good as a crow's or buzzard's.

The Duke looked up from where he lay on the ground. His back hurt. His feet and knees hurt. He stood up, winced, flung the black sack over his shoulder, and snuck off into the night.

Dweezil and Weezil stood in Queen Pixoratta's bedroom. Dweezil bent down, picked up the remnants of Pixoratta's yellow toenail, and turned it over between his fingers.

Sofia's Plan for Escape

THE FOLLOWING MORNING there was a large commotion at the castle. No one had seen a trace of Pixoratta, other than the bit of toenail on the floor, since the time she went to bed. Fluffles scurried about in search of their missing Queen, and Dweezil and Weezil, both preoccupied with the mysterious disappearance, failed to unlock Emmaline from her room.

Emmaline sat in the sad, empty room. She was very confused, as no one had bothered to mention to her that Pixoratta was missing. She was staring at the far wall when Sofia dropped from her hiding place in the ceiling and landed softly in front of her.

"Sofia! How did you get in here?"

Sofia pointed high up at a section of wall where a missing brick made a small hole where the wall met the ceiling.

"From up there," she said. "There was a loose brick, so I took it out and replaced it with a small board, which I painted gray. When I want to come in, I just move the board out of the way and drop down."

"Where does the hole go to?" asked Emmaline.

"To the room next to yours. It's just a regular bedroom, like this one used to be—no locks on the door, no bars on the windows. Once I'm in that room, I can get anywhere. I was thinking we could use it to get you out of here."

"I couldn't climb up to that opening. I don't have claws like you to grab on to the rock walls."

Sofia thought for a moment, then said, "What if I tie a rope to the bed in the other room? Then I could push the rope through the hole and you could use it to climb up and out to freedom."

"Oh, Sofia! That might work! Would you? Let's go now! I can't stand another minute here."

"No, not right now. Everyone is racing around looking for Pixoratta. She disappeared and you'd be captured before you made it past the hallway. No, we need to wait. Not tonight. They'll still be looking, but maybe tomorrow night, once things have calmed down."

"Why is everyone looking for Pixoratta? Where is she?"

"Didn't they tell you?"

"No. I've been locked in here all morning. No one has either come or gone."

"Well, Pixoratta disappeared last night. She just vanished. Everyone is looking for her. Dweezil found a toenail on the floor, but that's it."

"My heavens!" said Emmaline. She sighed, looked up at the hole in the wall, then said, "Sofia, why aren't you like the other Fluffles? You're fluffy and nice and sweet. Your fur is soft. You don't seem anything like them."

"Well—" She stopped. Her hair rose up slightly, then settled back down, before she continued. "I think it may have something to do with those green candies."

"What do you mean?"

"I think—" Sofia's fur stood straight up. She leapt towards the wall, scurried quickly, and dove through the hole. A small, wooden panel snapped into place over the opening, and although Emmaline had seen the whole thing, she no longer could tell where the solid wall ended and the fake panel began.

Keys jangled in the doorway. Dweezil came in, looking more miserable than ever. He shook a pitchfork at Emmaline. "Get up!" he barked. "Queen Bagalon wants you to check all the outhouses for Pixoratta. You've got work to do!"

Emmaline sat up, being careful to not look at the opening high in the wall, smoothed her tattered dress, and walked out of the room.

. . . But Not Forever

THE DUKE OF DUNGLEWOOD RODE HIS HORSE, Grayson, to the west, towards the Cliffs of Nomor. The sack holding the unconscious Pixoratta was tied to the saddle. At each stride, the bag swung out, paused in midair, and slammed back into the saddle, making a *clippity-clop-thud, clippity-clop-thud* sound. This continued for several hours before the Duke came to an intersection. To the left, a road continued uphill, into the clear skies surrounding the Cliffs of Nomor. The road to the right, however, was dark and foggy, unused and overgrown, and descended into the Swamps of Smugnuk. The Duke paused at the intersection and inspected both directions.

"Let's go have some fun in the swamp," he said.

Grayson shied from the path to the right. The Duke pulled hard on the reins and pointed his horse towards the swamp. Grayson turned a half circle and walked to the left.

"C'mon, Grayson! You know to behave better than that!" The Duke jerked the horse's head to the side. Grayson whinnied.

"I am the Duke of Dunglewood and you will do as I command!" the Duke shouted. He pointed Grayson in the right direction and whipped the horse in the rump with the flat of his sword. Grayson bolted forward, down the path, towards the Swamps of Smugnuk.

The fog was a swirling gray mist. It was hard for the Duke to see much past Grayson's nose. The world became the same shade of gray. Water dripped from the trees. Great, weeping vines hung from limbs. Ferns grew along the dark edges of the road. Brown bubbles formed and popped in the mud between trees. Slick moss covered the road and muffled the sounds of Grayson's horseshoes. No birds sang. No crickets chirped. The swamp breathed the gray insides of a crypt.

Grayson whinnied and shied away. He tugged at the reins. His legs trembled.

"Whoa, boy. Whoa!" Grayson stopped in the middle of the road and refused to move farther. "Fine. I guess here is as good a place as any."

The Duke slid off the saddle and stretched his arms. He took a few steps, loosening up the sore muscles in his legs, grabbed the sack from the saddle, and dropped it on the ground. He sliced the cord holding it shut and kicked the bag with his foot. Pixoratta, hardly looking like a Queen of anything, spilled forth. Her hair was matted and a bruise had formed over her left eye. She scampered three steps away from the Duke and stared up at him.

"Welcome to the Swamps of Smugnuk. Yes, scary isn't it? Oh, don't try to run away. Look around. Before you in every direction is swamp; you won't be going anywhere."

"Why—" Pixoratta began. She stopped at the sight of the Duke standing over her, his sword drawn from its scabbard.

"Why what? Why did I bring you here? It's very simple. My employer no longer has any need for you, and so I was hired to make you disappear." The Duke stroked a finger along the edge of his sword. "Forever."

"What? But I don't even know you! What could you have against me?"

"Ah, forgive me. I don't have anything against you at all. But, what I do have is a job to do, and what I enjoy more than anything else is doing my job. What is my job, you ask? Excellent question. I make people disappear. Forever. And it just so happens that today is your day to vanish." He waved the sword at the swamp. "I thought we would change things up a bit and let the swamp do the dirty work for me."

Queen Pixoratta looked at the bubbling mud in the mist.

"Go ahead. Hop on in. I'm sure it will feel like a nice mud bath, at least in the beginning. The mud will surround you and caress your skin and feel wonderful. Then you'll slowly sink down, farther and farther into the mud. Oh, don't try to struggle! Oh no. I hear that only makes it worse. No, just hop in, sink down, and relax in the mud as it fills your mouth and makes it impossible to scream—not that anyone would hear your screams out here anyway. Enjoy the swamp slowly filling your nose. Enjoy quietly suffocating. Perhaps you'll die before the top of your head dips below the surface, but then again, perhaps not. Oh, and don't forget the swampworms. They live in the swamp, crawl around in the mud, and spend all day waiting for someone to fall in. It takes a little while for them to find you, but when they do, oh, when they do. . . . They nibble your skin, eat your flesh—down to the bone—and then they eat the bone. Every last bit! So, drown in the swamp or get eaten by swampworms. It doesn't matter to me. Either way, you're dead! Oh, listen to me! I'm so excited! It feels like my birthday!"

The Duke of Dunglewood clapped his hands together then pointed the tip of his sword at the small Fluffle queen. Pixoratta scrambled backwards. Her clawed feet clutched at the ground but slid on slick ferns and wet moss-covered rocks.

"Now now, my little fuzzy friend. You're only making this harder on yourself," the Duke said. He stepped forward and lowered his sword closer to her face.

Queen Pixoratta grabbed a rotten stick and waved it the Duke. He swatted it from her hand with a small flick of his sword.

"Really? A twig? You're going to attack me with a twig? Oh, that is precious!" he snarled. "Now, I don't want to kill you, at least not with my sword. It's a very nice sword—my favorite actually—and I don't want your greasy fur to get stuck all over it. I don't mind the blood, but your fur is something else. So, instead, you need to jump in the swamp. Go ahead. Hop in. I have a very special reward waiting for me when I get back, so let's get this over with."

Pixoratta scrambled farther away. She grabbed a small rock and threw it at him. He knocked it to the side. He stepped closer, the tip of his sword only inches from her eyes. Mud squished against her heels. She scooped up a gob of the brown goo and threw it, hitting the Duke squarely in the face.

"Aigh! My eyes! My mustache! You got swamp mud in my mustache! That does it. No more Mr. Nice Guy!" The Duke wiped the swamp mud from his eyes and took a step towards Pixoratta, but the spot where she had been standing was empty. The Duke spun his head around, looking this way and that, before he found the small Fluffle sitting right above Grayson's tail. She held out a single finger, with one yellow claw at the end of it. She looked down at the Duke of Dunglewood and smiled.

"You disgusting monkey butt! How dare you throw mud at me! What are you smiling about? I should have thrown you in the swamp when you were in the sack, you infected tooth in a camel's tongue! But here I am, trying to be nice and let you enjoy getting killed, and you have to go and ruin it." He raised his sword and swung at Pixoratta.

Pixoratta leapt in the air. The sword swung harmlessly over Grayson's haunches and beneath Pixoratta's feet. The Duke swung again, and again, missed.

"You addle-brained oaf! Get back over here, you slimy baboon! I'll slice you in two!" He leapt in the air and swung with all his might. Had he connected with his intended target—Pixoratta's head—he surely would have split it in two, like a monkey splitting a banana, and she would have died right then and there. But Pixoratta, being a Fluffle (and a very nimble one at that), did two things. The first: she stepped sideways, off of Grayson's back, and slipped harmlessly underneath the Duke's sword. The second: on the way down, she poked her single, yellow fingernail into Grayson's rump in the exact same spot where the Duke had earlier smacked the poor horse with his sword. Grayson neighed loudly and kicked out both hind legs, connecting squarely with the Duke's chest. The Duke flew backwards, over wet rocks and the fallen log, and landed with a *slurp* and loud *oomph* in the swamp.

"Uuuuuuuuuuuugh . . . " said the Duke. He sat in the mud.

Grayson bolted, clattering down the path. He quickly vanished in the fog.

Pixoratta looked at the Duke. She tucked away her yellow claw and put her small hands on her hips.

"Uuuuuuuuuuuugh . . . uuuuuuugh . . . " The Duke of Dunglewood tried sit up, but his elbows sunk in the mud.

"What's that? I can't hear you, Duke. You need to talk louder," she said.

"Ugh . . . ooh . . . oh, my chest," the Duke wheezed.

"I bet that hurt. I've never been kicked by a horse before, but it sure looks painful."

The Duke look around and a sudden realization where he was came across his face. "Ooh. Help get me out of here," he said. His legs were slowly being sucked into the bog. He tried to push on the ground with his hand, but it too disappeared into the mud.

"What's that? You need to speak up. It's really hard to hear you."

"Ugh. Ow. I said, help me out of here! Throw me a rope from my saddlebag."

Pixoratta crossed her arms and tapped her foot. "You may not have noticed, since you just got kicked in the chest and all, but your horse ran off with the saddlebag."

"Then a stick, or something. Anything!" the Duke cried. He looked around frantically and stretched to grab a vine just out of reach over his head. Both of his legs disappeared as he sank lower into the muck.

Pixoratta found a small stick and waved it at him.

"You mean something like this, maybe?"

"Yes! Hold it over to me! Hurry! I'm sinking!"

"You mean hold it like this?" Pixoratta held the stick out in the air near the Duke's right hand. He reached out his arm as far as it would go and wrapped his fingers around the stick.

"Yes! Now pull!" he cried.

"You mean like this?" Pixoratta opened her fingers and dropped her end of the stick in the mud. It fell into the swamp and slowly sunk below the surface. "Whoops!" she said. "Must be my slimy baboon fingers. Sorry about that."

"You idiot! You can't drop the stick! What are you thinking? I could die out here!" screamed the Duke.

"That's *exactly* what I am thinking," said Pixoratta. She turned her back and started to walk away, leaving the Duke slowly sinking in the swamp.

"Where are you going? Get back here! Help me! I'm sinking!" The Duke twisted his head from side to side. His stomach, chest, and left hand were submerged in the mire. Small bubbles appeared where his body had been. "Ha ha! OK! You made your point! I'm sorry! Come back! We can work together! I promise! We can get revenge on Queen Bagalon, together! Just pull me out of the swamp!"

Pixoratta stopped and turned towards the Duke.

"Queen Bagalon? What does she have to do with this?" asked Pixoratta.

"She paid me to kill you! It was her idea. Honestly! I didn't want to, but she made me!"

"She made you? How?"

"She said she would give me a slave if I just did this one last thing for her."

"Really? A *slave*?"

"A slave, a wife, whatever! Honest!" He seeped farther down into the mud. Only his head and right arm cleared the surface. "I told her I had enough killing. 'No more!' I said. But she said, 'Just one more. You're the Duke of Dunglewood. Do this for me, and I'll find you the perfect wife.'" His eyes pleaded for Pixoratta to help him.

"You? *You're* the notorious Duke of Dunglewood? Well, well. How about that."

Pixoratta turned on her heel and started walking down the wet road, back the way they had come.

"Wait!" the Duke cried. "Come back here! I said I was sorry!"

Pixoratta didn't turn. She didn't flinch. She walked, away from the swamp, away from the Duke.

"Get back here, you disgusting maggot! Please! You lice-infected parasite! I'm asking nicely, you cabbage-eating, wart-covered, toad-spotted flap-dragon!" The Duke of Dunglewood smacked his right hand on the surface of the bog. He screamed and cursed and shook with fury. (Or at least the small part that hadn't been swallowed by the mud shook with fury.)

Without looking back, Pixoratta said, "Don't struggle, Dukie-boy. I hear that only makes it worse. Unless, of course, the swampworms get you first."

She walked down the road, through the gray mist, back towards the safety of solid ground.

The Duke's insults grew fainter and fainter, until they finally stopped completely.

Wedding Preparations

THE FOLLOWING DAY EMMALINE AWOKE with a start. She looked around her bedroom for Sofia, but found no one. Keys clattered in the lock, the door burst open, and Dweezil and Weezil strode into the room. Dweezil carried a pitchfork and a piece of white fabric, while Weezil carried two buckets and a large brush with hard bristles. It was the same brush Emmaline used to scrub the kitchen pots and pans. Dweezil poked Emmaline's leg with the pitchfork.

"Get on your feet, you lazy bum! It's time to get ready!" he said.

"Time to get ready for what?" Emmaline asked.

"Oh, it's your big day! A big celebration, today," hissed Weezil. He set one bucket on the ground, then pulled his arm back and threw the other bucket, filled with soapy water, on Emmaline's face.

"Ow! It burns! I can't see!" She raised her hands and rubbed her eyes. Weezil grabbed the large brush and scrubbed. The sharp bristles dug into her skin. Red welts soon crisscrossed Emmaline's back. She turned around. With one hand she rubbed her eyes and with the other she swatted at the painful bristles. Weezil was relentless.

"Gotta make you look nice for the big day. Queen's orders," said Dweezil. He poked Emmaline in the side with

the pitchfork, making her twist so Weezil could scrub a fresh section of skin.

"Wouldn't want her looking shabby today, would we Boss?" said Weezil.

"What's happening today? Why are you doing this?" Emmaline asked.

"It's your big day, stupid."

Weezil grabbed the second bucket and threw it. Emmaline gasped and clutched her arms close as cold water splashed over her. Soap bubbles flowed across the floor and formed a brown, frothy puddle near the bits of her mattress.

"My big day for what?"

"Only happens once, especially when the Duke's involved, so you gotta look nice," said Weezil. He grabbed Emmaline by the hair and yanked the bristle brush through it, pulling out large chunks of hair and snapping her head back with each stroke. Weezil stood back, reviewed his handiwork, and said, "Well, Boss, what do you think? She look magnificent enough?"

"A rat is a rat is a rat, no matter how long you bathe it."

"Maybe she could be the queen of the rats."

"Please, tell me," Emmaline said, "my big day for *what*?"

Dweezil and Weezil stopped what they were doing. Dweezil pointed at Emmaline and poked a yellow fingernail into her chest.

"Today, my dear, is your wedding day."

Emmaline gasped. "What? My *wedding* day? What are you talking about? It can't be my wedding day."

"Oh, but it is. Today's the day you marry the Duke of Dunglewood."

"The Duke of Dunglewood? I'm not marrying the Duke of Dunglewood!"

"Oh, yes you are. Queen's orders. She says you'll make the most magnificent bride."

Emmaline stood. Her arms hung limp next to her. She stared at the floor and shook her head. Weezil grabbed the white fabric from the ground while Dweezil yanked Emmaline's arms in the air. Emmaline shifted her gaze from the floor to the hole at the top of the wall. High in the shadows, she could barely make out a tuft of soft fur. Sofia's gentle brown eyes looked down at Emmaline, who mouthed the words *help me* before Weezil pulled the white dress over her arms and yanked it down. Emmaline's head popped through the top.

"Looks as good as we'll ever get it," said Dweezil.

Weezil inspected Emmaline. Her hair sagged down, tied in a clumsy knot behind her neck. The white dress, if you could call it that, hung from her body like shredded paper. Her arms, legs, and face were laced with red scratches.

"Aw, look at the pretty bride—she's blushing, Boss."

"And crying too. No doubt with joy."

"Yes, but something's missing . . ."

"I think the bride needs some flowers for her hair, don't you?"

"Flowers! That's it!"

Weezil bent down, tore out a handful of straw from Emmaline's mattress and shoved it behind her ear.

"Oh! So much better! She could be in a rat beauty pageant!" Dweezil and Weezil laughed. They grabbed Emmaline's arms and marched her out the door.

They did not see the secret panel close shut over the hole high in the wall.

The Wedding

OUTSIDE, THE DAY WAS CRISP AND CLEAR. A few white clouds dotted the blue sky as if they had appeared for the sole purpose of making Emmaline's wedding that much more beautiful. The bright sun blinded Emmaline as she stepped out onto the castle steps leading down to the main square. She raised an arm and shielded her eyes.

"That's right. Wave to all the pretty people," said Dweezil, who clutched Emmaline by the arm.

Emmaline's eyes adjusted to the light. The townspeople, dressed in their finest, filled the main square. Greasy Fluffles, wearing ill-fitting coats and brightly-colored dresses, darted in and out of the crowd.

"Keep moving, brat."

"And don't forget to smile. It's your wedding day after all."

Dweezil and Weezil pushed her down the steps. They waved and smiled at the crowd. None of the townspeople cheered. They looked sullen, downtrodden, crushed. Fluffles, on the other hand, danced about and shouted. Emmaline staggered forward. Her arms hung by her sides; her blank face stared out. Every so often she would shake her head from side to side as if she were trying to figure out which foot was supposed to move next. As the small group reached the bottom of the steps, the crowd parted and made a pathway from the castle to the far side of the grassy square where the large elegant cathedral stood. Ornate spires rose high into the sky. Stone columns with statues of famous kings and queens adorned the nooks between arched windows. Thirty peaks dotted the roofline, and the main spire ascended higher than even the decorative clouds. At its top, a green flag bordered with golden lilies, a tradition reserved only for weddings, flew in the breeze.

Emmaline pushed one foot in front of the other, walking slowly, as if in a trance, but was still surprised when she reached the large wooden doors of the cathedral. Glancing up, she saw the newly erected gold statue of Queen Bagalon in the main archway. Behind it, Emmaline could make out the faded stones in the shape of the shadow of King Zantavi's statue which had occupied that particular space for the previous five hundred years.

Emmaline walked into the cathedral. The stained-glass windows cast rainbows of color across stone columns along either side of the main hallway. A wide, red velvet carpet lay between rows of wooden pews filled with townspeople and Fluffles. The townspeople sat with their hands folded in their laps. The Fluffles leapt from pew to pew, crawled under benches, and played hide-and-seek behind large vases filled with flowers.

Several steps led up to a platform at the far end of the cathedral, where a priest waited. He wore long white robes and a tall hat. A green band of velvet draped over his shoulders. Behind him, on her own platform two steps higher, Queen Bagalon sat in a golden throne. Her staff, with the gray stone laced in vines at its end, leaned against an armrest. The priest saw Emmaline, glanced at the orchestra, and nodded. Music filled the enormous room.

"C'mon, buttercup. Get marching," said Dweezil. He thrust his pitchfork in Emmaline's back. She lurched forward, regained her balance, and walked down the aisle. Heads turned as she walked past, following her deathly march to the front of the cathedral. She felt the soft velvet carpet on her bare feet and squeezed the fibers between her toes. *This is not how my wedding is supposed to be*, she thought.

She passed the final pew where Dweezil and Weezil dropped their grip on her arms but not on their pitchforks. The priest motioned for Emmaline to take her place next to him. She walked up three steps—three steps closer to her grave—stepped to the left, and turned to face the congregation. A tear rolled down her cheek. The priest smiled at her. From her throne in the back, Queen Bagalon beamed.

Emmaline sighed and looked towards the ceiling. Wooden rafters crisscrossed high in the air above the cathedral's open floor. Beams were notched together and pegged with wooden pins, and, just above the pins, was something not-quite-right. Something out of place. Something . . . fuzzy.

"Sofia?" Emmaline whispered as she squinted at the rafters.

"Such a beautiful bride. Doesn't she look lovely?" Queen Bagalon said.

The large bells at the top of the cathedral rang out.

"Oh, right on time!" said Queen Bagalon. She clapped her hands together and sat up in her throne.

Trumpets blared.

Fluffles jumped up on top of pews and climbed flower vases.

Townspeople turned and looked at the main door, waiting to catch a glimpse of the notorious Duke of Dunglewood.

But the Duke did not appear.

The church was silent. Queen Bagalon pinched her eyebrows together. She waved her hand in a small circle at the trumpeters. They raised their trumpets and played a second fanfare.

But again, the Duke did not appear. The door to the cathedral remained empty. Hushed comments swirled around the church like small breezes.

Queen Bagalon leaned over and whispered to Dweezil, "Where is the Duke? He's supposed to be here. Exactly at noon is what he said." Dweezil shrugged and put his hands in the air.

From outside the cathedral, metal clanged on stone. A guard wearing armor and holding the handle of his sword appeared in the doorway. He half strode, half ran down the center aisle, clanking and rattling with each step. He climbed the steps, hurried past Emmaline, past the priest, and stopped in front of Queen Bagalon. He bent down on one knee and gasped for air. His chest heaved.

"Your Highness," he said. His words echoed in the still hall.

"Yes. Proceed," she replied.

"The Duke of Dunglewood is missing."

A gasp arose from the townspeople.

"What do you mean, *missing*? Where is the Duke? He is supposed to be here! He's getting married, for heaven's sake!"

"We don't know where he is for certain, your Highness. His horse appeared at the castle gates with its saddle still on, but the Duke wasn't with it. We feel certain he was at the Swamps of Smugnuk. A traveler found his sword by the edge of the swamp, and we found swamp mud on the back of the horse. We've been searching, but—"

"But what? Spit it out, man! But what?"

"But, we think the Duke is dead. If he fell in the swamp, there is no way he would have survived."

Queen Bagalon jumped out of her throne, leaving her staff behind. Her face was contorted in anger. Her lips pulled back as she pointed a finger at Emmaline.

"YOU IMPERTINENT BEAST! How dare you do this to me, Emmaline! You horrible creature!" Queen Bagalon's body shook with rage.

"Wha—? What did I do?" Emmaline asked.

"What did you do? What did you do? You *killed* the Duke to keep him from coming to his own wedding, you miserable brute."

"How could I have done that?"

"I put together this lovely wedding, invited all these people, filled the church with flowers, and you, you ungrateful wretch, ruined it! You killed your husband! On your wedding day no less! Guards! Seize her! She's a murderer! Prepare the gallows!"

Dweezil looked at Weezil, and both grinned. They lowered their pitchforks. Emmaline was trapped—the Queen in front of her, Dweezil to her right, Weezil to her left, the armed guard, the townspeople and the Fluffles behind her. There was nowhere for her to run.

From high in the rafters, where two beams crossed, came a blood-curdling scream. Sofia's sharp claws popped out of her fingers as she leapt from her hiding spot.

The Escape

SOFIA'S SCREAM WAS AS TERRIFYING A SCREAM as you have ever heard. The townspeople's eyes popped open. The hair on the Fluffles backs stood on end. Dweezil and Weezil clutched their pitchforks tightly.

Sofia landed on the dais next to where Bagalon had been sitting. She grabbed Bagalon's staff from its resting place against the throne, and swung, hard, hitting Dweezil in the back of his knee. The greasy Fluffle toppled backwards to the floor. Sofia swung in the other direction and caught Weezil in the back of his head. His eyes crossed. He dropped his pitchfork and tumbled forward. Dweezil sat up and Sofia smacked him on the head with the staff. Dweezil fell sideways and lay still. Sofia jumped in front of Emmaline and pointed the end of the scepter at Queen Bagalon's head.

"Really?" said Queen Bagalon, who had become very calm, eerily serene.

Sofia didn't say anything. She put out a small arm and pushed Emmaline farther behind her, farther away from the Queen, towards the back of the church.

"You can't protect her. You know that, don't you?" said Bagalon.

Sofia clung to the scepter. She thrust the stone towards Bagalon's face, but the Queen merely smiled.

"You think you can jump in, wave my staff around, and save your little friend who just ruined her own wedding? Well, I have news for you. It won't happen. Listen up and listen well. I'm going to just say one thing and one thing only: *Boram ipsula flom bipsum!*"

The stone in the staff began to glow red, faintly at first, then slowly it became brighter until it looked like a large ruby. Swirls of black smoke danced inside the gem. Sofia blinked twice. The people around her faded. The Fluffles, the room, the grand ceiling, all faded. Sofia's eyes stared at the glowing stone filled with spinning smoke.

"Pretty, isn't it?" said Queen Bagalon. "It's the scepter of Tar-Aloon. You remember Tar-Aloon, don't you? He lived inside a volcano. They say he could turn rocks into fire. *Flob smipsum bas fazzah!*" A thunderstorm of gray smoke billowed inside the ruby. Bright red rays of light radiated out. Sofia squinted, transfixed by the heat and glowing light.

"That's right. Look at the pretty fire. Watch the smoke swirl. It's beautiful. So beautiful. . . ."

Sofia's bottom jaw sagged. She loosened her grip on the staff.

Bagalon stepped closer.

"Good girl. Now put my staff down." Bagalon said. Her voice was a cool breeze to the fire burning in Sofia's eyes.

Sofia's arms drooped and the end of the staff sunk towards the floor.

"No!" screamed Emmaline. She jumped forward and grabbed the staff from Sofia's hands at the same time Queen Bagalon reached for the end with the glowing red stone in it, but Emmaline was faster. The Queen's hand grabbed empty air as Emmaline swung the scepter of Tar-Aloon above her head and down into the tile floor shattering the glowing stone. A scarlet bolt of lightning burst forth and a tremendous thunderclap cracked. Black smoke filled the room. Bright red shards of broken glass scattered, cooled, and turned to stone on the floor.

Sofia blinked, as if waking from a dream. She shook her head twice and saw Emmaline reeling from the sudden blast.

Bagalon dove to the floor. She crawled on her hands and knees trying to scoop together bits of Tar-Aloon's broken stone. Blood trickled between her fingers where the stone fragments cut her flesh. "No! No! No! This can't be happening!" Bagalon cried.

Sofia grabbed Emmaline's hand. "Run, Emmaline! Run!"

She pulled Emmaline past Queen Bagalon to the back of the church, opened a door and the two staggered into a hallway. They turned left, ran down the hallway, came to an intersection, and turned right, then left again. They stopped and looked at a large staircase leading up in front of them.

Bagalon stared at her hand. Small streams of blood dripped between her fingers and onto the floor, mixing with the stone splinters. She pulled a small gray fragment, sharp, with stinging edges, from between her fingers and held her hand to her chest. More blood dripped onto the floor. She furrowed her brow, shook her head from side to side, and looked out at the dazed faces.

"GO GET THEM, YOU FOOLS! DON'T LET THEM ESCAPE!"

The Fluffles, hundreds of them, grabbed their pitchforks (yes—they even brought their pitchforks to a wedding) and chased after Emmaline and Sofia like a seething tidal wave of greasy fur. The first to arrive in the hallway stopped, sniffed the air, wolf-like, and pointed to the left. The mass of dark fur, yellow talons, and sharp teeth, churned down the hall after Emmaline and Sofia.

At the base of the staircase, Sofia heard the clamor of claws on stone. "Hurry!" she cried, pulling Emmaline's hand. They raced up the steps, down another hallway, up a second flight of stairs, through a wooden door, and into the priest's apartment above the church. Sofia slammed the door shut behind them and turned the key in the lock.

Emmaline looked around the ornate room—a large wooden desk with papers on it, a quill and inkwell, sofas, a stone fireplace with embers and ash, long velvet drapes on either side of the windows; in a side room through an open archway—a bed with a soft red comforter, dozens of pillows, an armoire with a wide drawer at the bottom, a chevalier mirror in front of a large tapestry, and a chamber pot. (If you don't know what a chamber pot is, let me explain. Before there were toilets, before indoor plumbing or bathrooms, there were chamber pots, which were simply buckets people used to take care of their "private needs" in middle of the night. Their private needs stayed in the chamber pot until the morning, when a chamber maid, who had the worst job ever, threw the stinky contents of the pot out the window.)

Emmaline raced to the side room and dove under the bed. She peeked out from under the edge of the soft quilt and called up to Sofia. "Quick! Hide under here with me!"

Back in the hallway, the pack of Fluffles raced through the corridor, bounced off walls, and leapt off furniture. They ran up the stairs and crashed into the apartment door.

Next to the bed, Sofia bent down, grabbed Emmaline by the wrist, and pulled. "We can't hide here!" cried Sofia.

Emmaline braced her foot against the bedframe. "Yes we can! Leave me alone!"

"No, they will find us and they will kill us." Sofia loosened her grip on Emmaline's wrist. "I know a way. You need to trust me." Her brown eyes, full of concern, pleaded.

Emmaline hesitated. She heard Fluffles howling and scratching at the locked door. From her spot underneath the bed, she saw the door shake and tremble. Claws ripped at the bottom, tearing out chunks of wood. Soon, the door would no longer be a door, but merely a pile of toothpick-sized bits of wood. Emmaline wriggled out from underneath the bed.

Sofia pointed across the room at the large tapestry. "There's a hidden door. It's hard to find—crawl behind the tapestry. There's a small hole near the floor, no bigger than a mouse hole. Put your hand in it. There's a latch on the right side. Push on the latch and the door will open. I'll be right behind you."

"Wait, there's a hidden—"

"Go!" Sofia pushed Emmaline towards the tapestry. Emmaline staggered forward, ran past the mirror, and ducked under the ornate rug. From where Sofia stood, it appeared as if Emmaline were a large lump, an enormous mouse, crawling behind the curtain. The lump bent down, crawled some more, stopped, clicked, squeaked, and vanished. A faint breeze of fresh air stirred in the room.

Sofia, on the other hand, could only have been described as a small fluffy brown hurricane. She jumped on top of the bed, slid under the sheets, and rolled around. She climbed up the armoire, scooted across the top, scrabbled down the other side, opened the large drawer at the base, dove in, and leapt out. She ran into the other room, climbed up and down every drape, sped over to the desk, jumped in one drawer and came out another, crawled under the rug, skipped across the mantle, leapt onto the chandelier, swung back into the bedroom, circled the mirror three times, picked up the chamber pot, ran underneath it, and ducked behind the large tapestry, where she looked like a small lump or an enormous-but-not-so-enormous mouse.

Click, squeak, swish. A faint breeze and the second lump disappeared.

The tapestry settled back into place.

The bedroom was quiet for one long second until the door splintered apart. Dweezil, then Weezil, then the pack of greasy Fluffles poured in from the hallway like oil spilling over a dam. They raced in, pitchforks ready.

"She's under the bed! I can smell her!" said one.

"They're under the sheets!" said another.

"They went in the armoire!"

"I smell her behind the curtains!"

". . . in the desk!"

". . . under the rug!"

". . . over the mantle!"

". . . on the chandelier!"

". . . under the chamber pot!"

Fluffle noses sniffed voraciously as their arms whirled and claws shredded each and every place Sofia had run. The bedsheets were clawed to ribbons. The legs of the bed ripped to dust. The armoire split open; the drawer thrown across the room and smashed; the curtains yanked from curtain rods. The desk exploded into shards of wood, paper, and ink. The mantle, clawed and scratched, turned into a diving board for three Fluffles who, having launched themselves into the air, were spinning in circles on the great chandelier. Even the chamber pot—the chamber pot!—was thrown in the air, flipped several times, and smashed on the ground, spilling some very unmentionable, and very unpleasant, "private needs" everywhere.

Soon the cacophony stopped.

Dweezil looked around the room. Destruction. Locked windows.

"Where are they?" he shouted.

The Fluffles looked at each other, confused.

"They couldn't have just disappeared!" boomed Dweezil. Furiously, he grabbed the tapestry on the wall, ripped it down, and started to throw it across the room, but stopped. He sniffed the back, down low. He breathed in a second time, this time holding the fabric close to his nose. He turned, looked at the empty wall in front of him, spotted the small hole near the floor, bent down on his knees, and stuck a yellow fingernail into the opening. He wiggled his finger and heard a *click*. A section of the wall opened. A long rooftop walkway appeared on the other side.

It was not like a walkway you might see today. No, the cathedral roofs were cliff-like; the walkway was no wider than a banana laid sideways. There was no railing and the edge of the walkway vanished into the space between the cathedral and the flying buttresses, where, far down below, stone paths sleepily waited to put an end to anyone unfortunate enough to fall from such a great height. At the far end of the roof, the central tower, a circular masterpiece of stone and marble, rose high above all the other spires. And just at its base, where the rooftop met the tower, Dweezil saw Emmaline crawling on her hands and knees.

Sofia urged Emmaline forward, towards a door tucked into the tower's side.

"I can't go on," Emmaline said. Her lungs tightened. It was hard for her to breathe. Her stomach felt like churned cabbages. A strong wind whistled past.

"You must. Only a little bit farther." Sofia looked back the way they had come. Dweezil stepped through the hidden door, pointed at them, and shouted something that was caught and whisked away by the wind. The horde of Fluffles scurried out the door and ran along the rooftop towards them. "Hurry!" Sofia cried. She opened the door to the great spire.

Emmaline inched forward, slowly.

The Fluffles raced towards them, seemingly unaware of the great height. They dug their claws into the roof as if it were made of soft dirt. Tiles broke off, slid down, and spilled over the edge.

Sofia grabbed Emmaline, pulled her through the doorway and onto a small platform. She slammed the door behind them. "No time to catch your breath!" Three points of a pitchfork *thunked* through the door near her head.

The inside of the tower resembled a hollow tube standing on end. As the tower was meant for decoration and not really visitors, nothing had been done to make it safe. Small, uneven steps with no handrail jutted out from the sides of the walls and spiraled up and down the tower's insides. The center of the tower was nothing more than one long hole down to the base of the cathedral. Other than a few small window slits, it was unadorned.

Emmaline pressed her body against the wall and tried, as best she could, not to look down. Sofia pushed the small girl forwards, up the stairs. They climbed, making smaller and smaller circles towards the top.

"Shouldn't we be heading *down*?" asked Emmaline. "How are we going to get away from them? There's nowhere for us to go up there."

Sofia started to answer when the door below them slammed open. Sofia looked back and made out the shapes of Fluffles running up the stairs, leaping across the spire's center hole, grabbing steps with their hands, clawing over each other to chase them. Sofia pushed Emmaline forward, towards the topmost step and a small door, through the door, then out onto a small ledge with a tiny railing at the very top of the main spire. Emmaline saw the Montagalla Mountains far to the south, the Sea of Trancilee to the north, and, to the west, the tall Cliffs of Nomor and the foggy gray blackness perpetually surrounding the Swamps of Smugnuk. Far below the two escapees, looking like small ants, townspeople dotted the main square between the cathedral and the castle. At this height, the wind whipped like a raging river.

"Climb up here," Sofia said as she leapt onto the parapet.

"What are you doing? You could fall!"

"I won't fall. Now climb up here and grab my ankles. Hurry!"

Sounds of angry Fluffles running up the tower stairs echoed through the doorway. Emmaline put one hand on the wall, pushed a knee next to it, then pulled her body up. She stood, on the balcony wall, at the top of the tallest spire of the cathedral, and tried not to cry.

"Now grab my ankles. Grab on as hard as you can. Your life depends on it."

Emmaline slid her hands over Sofia's hairy feet and grabbed her ankles.

Sofia bent her knees, locked her hands over Emmaline's, and jumped. Not up, but out. Out over the edge of the wall. Out into the great void, pulling Emmaline with her. Emmaline found herself at the same time both hanging from Sofia's ankles and falling to her death. The two tumbled in the air as they plummeted towards the ground. Then, Sofia gulped a big mouthful of air and sneezed, but didn't. It was the kind of sneeze that shows up while you're watching a movie in a theater or eating at a fine restaurant, and, in order to not make noise, you keep your mouth shut, so instead of a loud *achoo!* sound you end up making a *ka-snork* sound and you feel like your eyes are going to pop out of your head and your nose is going to explode. It was a sneeze like that. At exactly the *ka-snork* moment, Sofia's fluffy fur stood on end and popped out, as if it had grown three times as long and nine times as fluffy. The wind caught her long soft hairs, and, looking like a dandelion in full bloom, Sofia and Emmaline gently floated away.

Dweezil, then Weezil, then the pack of Fluffles burst out onto the ledge at the top of the spire. They yelled. They threw pitchforks. They gulped big mouthfuls of air, appeared to sneeze and made *ka-snork* sounds. But their greasy fur didn't pop out or turn them into giant puffballs. Their fur clung together in slimy mats and twitched.

Dweezil clenched his teeth. His hands clutched the sides of the wall and squeezed. The stone crumbled between his fingers as he watched Sofia and Emmaline drift away over the castle walls.

Return to the Swamps of Smugnuk

EMMALINE HELD ON TO SOFIA'S ANKLES and drifted with the wind. The tall spire receded behind them, as did the cathedral, the castle, and finally the town. They would sometimes descend towards the ground, then a gust of wind would push them high up in the air, spin them around a few times, and leave them floating even higher. The skies to the north darkened. The gusts of wind became more fierce, and colder too. A light rain started to fall.

"Sofia, can we go down? My hands are starting to hurt."

"I can't control where we go. We can only go where the wind takes us. Pretend you're a cottonwood seed." She had to speak loudly to be heard over the wind.

"How long do you think we'll be up here?" Emmaline asked.

"I don't know. Ask the wind."

"It doesn't seem like the wind is very interested in talking."

Indeed, the wind was not interested in discussing anything with the floating travelers. It shouted at them, screamed, and didn't care if they were having a nice flight; it pummeled them, pushing them back and forth in the air. The rain came faster, cold and stinging. Water dripped down

Emmaline's hair. Sofia pulled her ankles up into her body, lifting Emmaline into her soft fur, and, if not keeping her dry, managed to make her a little less miserable.

"I'm r-r-really getting cold, Sofia. Are you sure we c-c-can't land somewhere?"

"We're getting lower, but if I pull my fur in, we'll plummet to the ground. You need to hold on."

"M-maybe you could pull your fur in just a little."

"Maybe," said Sofia, "but I don't think so. We can't land here anyway. Look down."

Emmaline had kept her eyes closed against the rain, but now she opened them. She looked out, and saw, far to the east, the faintest trace of the castle. The two had drifted westward. She looked down, and realized they were floating directly over the foggy blackness surrounding the Swamps of Smugnuk. She closed her eyes. The last rays of light vanished as black clouds from the north erased the setting sun.

The rain intensified. It slashed at her face, arms, and legs.

Night settled in. Blackness surrounded them.

The wind, laughingly, pushed them skyward, dropped them towards the earth, swept them sideways, and rolled them through the air like a cat playing with a small mouse. Every so often it would pause, just long enough to give them hope, then it would bat them through the air, chase them, claw at their legs, toss them between the dark clouds, and start over.

Emmaline felt a rip at her leg. A branch hidden in the darkness. A second slash and then Emmaline was torn from Sofia, lost in the darkness. Leaves and needles tore at her arms and legs and hands and face. She tumbled down through sharp branches and crashed into the ground. She grunted, once, then lay still.

Hiding in the Swamp

THE RAIN CONTINUED THROUGH THE NIGHT, then let up slightly as the sun rose, and stopped completely by midmorning. The clouds dissipated, breaking off into small groups and wandered home, like guests after a party. The sun shone through a blue sky and did its best to dry out the grass, trees, and weary travelers. Emmaline slept and dreamed she was wrapped in a white blanket. The fabric glowed, a peaceful glow, as if it were woven from the light of a dozen candles. The light surrounded her. She drifted in the whiteness. From above, or below, or perhaps somewhere else, someone, or something, or maybe nothing at all, called her name. It wasn't a sound so much as a thought, the idea of her name being called.

Emmaline ignored it. She drifted. The blanket was both a warm cloud floating in the heavens and a soft flat-bottomed boat, quilted with swan feathers, floating down a calm river in the sunshine.

"Emmaline."

A voice, this time a real voice, came from the milky white sky of her dream. It was impossible to ignore, but Emmaline did her best to ignore it anyway. In her dream she floated, back on the boat of feathers. A small wave hit the side of the boat. Water splashed on her face. The boat rocked.

"Emmaline."

The voice again, hushed, but urgent. Another wave, this time larger, shook her feathery boat. Emmaline, eyes closed, reached out to steady herself. She grabbed handfuls of feathers, dropped them, and tried again, only to have her arms push through the sides of the boat. Feathers peeled away like sand blown down a beach. The feathers whipped her face. She felt a wetness on her back. *That's odd*, she thought. *I wonder if the boat is leaking?*

Another wave crashed over her. Feathers stuck to Emmaline's face. She sunk below the water's surface, unable to breathe. Bubbles from her mouth drifted up to the feathers—millions of white feathers now—covering the surface above her. As she watched, the feathers turned silver, then gray, then black. From the blackness a face appeared. A familiar face. Sofia's face.

"Emmaline!" Sofia hissed.

Emmaline opened her eyes. She gasped for air, but Sofia's hand was clamped tightly over her mouth.

"Hush!" The tone of Sofia's voice was enough to wake Emmaline, but it was the fear in her eyes that made Emmaline stop struggling.

Sofia relaxed her grip. She lay on top of Emmaline, underneath three pine trees at the edge of a forest. Her fur was long, fluffed out, and covered Emmaline's body. To their left, trees grew in thick numbers and faded into darkness. To their right, a wide green field lay between the woods and the base of a cliff. A small road, a path stretching between the woods and mountain, wound across the field in either direction. Six armored horsemen rode in three rows of two down the path. Horses' tails swished as they trotted farther and farther away. Sofia watched the men intently. As did the creature on their left.

Emmaline recognized the emblems on the riders' backs.

"Those are—" Emmaline started to say.

"Shh!" the creature said. Sofia slapped a hand back over Emmaline's mouth. Emmaline relaxed. She put her head back and rested on a pillow of pine needles. Her body hurt. Her leg hurt. Her head pounded. Her mouth tasted like dried dirt. She closed her eyes and tried to go back to the warm blanket of light. The boat of white feathers.

A body next to her moved. "I think they're gone," it said, then added, "but they'll be back."

Sofia rolled off Emmaline. "It's OK. You can open your eyes now." Her tiny voice was a bell. Behind closed eyes, Emmaline watched the feather boat sail off without her. She opened her eyes and looked into Sofia's face. A second face appeared.

Emmaline looked at the face. She recognized the face. It was a face that had gone missing. It was even rumored that the face, that particular face, belonged to a dead Fluffle.

"Pixoratta?" Emmaline asked.

The face was indeed Pixoratta's and she was indeed quite alive. Her fur was matted, caked in swamp mud. Her bloodshot eyes, a strange combination of yellow and white, sagged. Her claws were greenish-yellow at the tips, but a light yellow, almost cream color, near her hands. And she was alive.

"You're alive!"

"Yes, Emmaline, I'm alive. And yes, those were guards from the castle we just watched ride past."

"Why didn't you stop them?" Emmaline asked. She looked at both Sofia and Pixoratta. "They could have helped us get back."

"Why didn't we stop them?" Sofia asked. "Why didn't we stop them? Don't you remember? They wanted to kill us. Queen Bagalon wants us captured. Or killed."

Emmaline stared at the pine trees above her. Sunlight and blue sky peeked through the needles. She realized she was hungry, tried to sit up, felt a sharp pain in her side, near the base of her ribcage, and lay back down.

"Shh, relax. You've had a pretty hard fall."

"And a pretty hard nap too."

"How long have I been asleep?" Emmaline asked. From the sun, she could tell it was midmorning, but with the headache and trees, she wasn't exactly sure what hour it was.

"Five days," said Sofia.

"*Five days?*" Emmaline replied. "How is that possible?"

"You hit your head on a branch when we crashed. You've been asleep ever since."

"My head does hurt. And I'm pretty hungry. Five days? Really?"

"Yes, five days. You haven't eaten in five days. Pixoratta hasn't eaten in almost twelve."

Emmaline looked at Pixoratta. She had lost weight. Even through the fur, Emmaline saw her skin was sagging. Emmaline patted her dress. "I don't have any food, but I think I have a piece of candy in my pocket—"

A sudden change came over Pixoratta. Her eyes widened, her lips pulled back, and her teeth gnashed. "CANDY!" she yelled. "CANDY! CANDY! GIMME CANDY!"

Sofia grabbed Emmaline's pocket, and tore it—with the candy inside—right off Emmaline's dress. She jumped over Emmaline's body, ran several steps away, turned to face them, and crouched. Pixoratta jumped up from where she had been sitting, winced, and fell to the ground. Her breathing slowed and the sudden change that had come over her quickly disappeared.

"No! No candy! No one gets any candy!" said Sofia, as she tucked the fabric and candy away, somewhere inside her fur.

"But Fluffles love candy," said Emmaline.

Pixoratta rolled over from where she had fallen. "No. Sofia's right. There's something wrong with that candy," she sighed. "It makes me sick. No candy. Not for me. Not for anyone."

"I don't understand," said Emmaline.

"We think the candy's poisoned," said Sofia. "Bagalon's been using it to control the Fluffles."

"My goodness! Poisoned? I just thought Fluffles really liked it."

Pixoratta paused, thought for a second, and then asked, "Emmaline, do you think Fluffles are mean, nasty creatures?"

"Well, I wouldn't say *mean*. Perhaps *rude*, but not mean."

"What about when Dweezil and Weezil poked you with a pitchfork, locked you in room, and didn't let you out and poured soapy water in your eyes and brushed your hair with a bristle brush from the kitchen? What about then?"

"I don't know. I guess they were doing their job."

"They're my assistants, not Bagalon's thugs. They're supposed to help me."

"Well, I guess they can be pretty mean."

"And what about Sofia? Is she nasty?"

"Heaven's no! Sofia is wonderful. She's very sweet. She's my friend."

"And look at her fur. It isn't greasy. It's fluffy, like a Fluffle's fur is supposed to be. How do you think we got the name Fluffles? Sofia's eyes are brown, not yellow, and her claws are smooth and white. Look at my claws—cracked, broken, yellow, and smelly! And, do you know what else is different about Sofia? She was the only Fluffle to not eat the candy. Everyone else ate it and they started getting greasy and playing mean tricks on each other. Our nails changed shape and color. Even our eyes changed," said Pixoratta. She lay back, tired.

Sofia walked back over to the two and sat down on the pine needles next to Emmaline. "I got scared around them. You saw Dweezil and Weezil—they ate the most candy of anyone. So, I ran away and hid in the castle."

"Which, in all likelihood, was the best thing you could have done," said Pixoratta.

"It sounds terrible." said Emmaline. "I knew Bagalon could be mean, but I had no idea. To imagine, she might be poisoning you. And to think I helped. Oh my! I'm so sorry I gave you candy! I didn't know!" Emmaline sat up, bent forward to give Pixoratta a hug, threw both hands around the Fluffle queen, and shrieked, "AIGH! PIXORATTA! WHERE'S YOUR FOOT?"

Emmaline stared at Pixoratta's legs. Both were furry; both were brown; both were caked in swamp mud, but only one had a foot at the end of it. The other—which Emmaline was certain had a foot on it the last time they were together—did not. The other leg ended in a stump. In precisely zero-point-zero-two seconds, Emmaline had completely forgotten about the possibly poisoned candy and could only think of Pixoratta's missing foot.

Pixoratta raised her leg—the footless leg—and wiggled her toes in the air, only there weren't any toes, so she just held her leg in the air and looked at where her toes would have been.

"Ah, yes. The swampworms of Smugnuk." She stopped trying to wiggle her phantom foot and rested her leg back on the ground. "Quite a long story, but I'll do my best." She told Emmaline about being captured by the Duke of Dunglewood, about how the Queen had hired him, about how he had tied her up in a sack and dragged her to the Swamps of Smugnuk; about how he had held her at sword-point, and about how Grayson the horse had kicked the dreadful Duke of Dunglewood to a murky demise.

Emmaline grimaced. "Did he cut your foot off before the horse kicked him? How did you jump off with only one foot?"

"No, he didn't get near me with his sword, although he probably thought he did."

"But what happened to your foot?"

"I had to get back to help the Fluffles, *my Fluffles*. So I walked. All day and into the night. I should have stopped when it got dark, but I didn't. I was still crazy from the candy and nearly being killed by the Duke. I wasn't thinking right. I stepped off the path and my foot squished down into the swamp. I grabbed a tree branch, which kept me from falling all the way in, and, luckily, held on. But I couldn't pull my foot out of the muck. And trust me, I tried. I pushed the ground with my good leg. I pulled the branch with my arms. Nothing worked. I was stuck. I stood in that spot all night long and held onto the branch for fourteen hours—well into the next day. That's when the swampworms showed up. I felt something below my foot, a tickle at first, and then a tiny bite—I could barely feel it—and then another, and another and then it felt like my whole foot was on fire. Before I knew what happened, the swampworms had eaten my foot clean off. The entire foot. Gone."

"Oh my gosh! That's horrible!" Emmaline said.

"Yes. But also, no," Pixoratta replied.

"What do you mean, *also no*? They ate your foot! How is it anything but horrible?"

"Well, with no foot, I didn't have a foot stuck in the mud anymore. I could get away. I crawled and hopped on one foot until I passed out. If it hadn't been for the swampworms eating my foot and getting me unstuck from the swamp, I'd still be hanging on to that tree branch. Or I would've let go and died in the swamp. So, in a way, the swampworms saved my life."

Emmaline thought about it. It still sounded horrible, but maybe not. She wasn't sure.

"I found Pixoratta near the entrance to the swamp four days ago," Sofia said. "I brought her back here."

"And thank you for doing that," Pixoratta said. She patted Sofia's hand. "Queen Bagalon's patrols have been riding up and down the countryside looking for us. And, you know what else? If I hadn't gotten stuck in the mud, I would've been out of the swamp fourteen hours sooner. Sofia wouldn't have found me and I would've been out in the open fields when the patrols arrived, and they would have found me in no time. So, in a way, sticking my foot in the swamp saved my life twice. It just may have been the luckiest thing ever to happen to me."

Emmaline sat and thought. And no matter how many times she thought about it, no matter how many ways she ran it through her head, she still thought having her foot eaten by swampworms would be horrible.

The odd trio, Emmaline, Sofia, and Pixoratta, sat under the pine trees and talked through the afternoon. Emmaline told Pixoratta about her forced marriage to the dreadful Duke of Dunglewood (a failed marriage, thankfully), and about smashing the scepter of Tar-Aloon, and how she and Sofia ran for their lives, didn't hide under a bed, and drifted through a horrible thunderstorm to arrive where they found themselves now. All of which Pixoratta had heard from Sofia days before while Emmaline slept, but she listened intently to Emmaline's story nonetheless.

They talked about the townspeople, how their faces were sunken and hollow. How they moved slowly, with their heads down, and how they shuffled their feet; how Davinda only jumped off the diving board and didn't do flips anymore; how Bella only lifted small weights and how Humungo spent all his time at his forge, making small, Fluffle-sized pitchforks; how the Baker's donuts were not so doughy and how the Baker's Husband had become so thin; how the small man with the round glasses hadn't been able to find his glasses in months; and how the Jeweler only made teardrop necklaces.

They talked about the Fluffles. About how Dweezil and Weezil were so absolutely awful. (They hadn't always been that way, Pixoratta assured Emmaline.) How the Fluffles' fur had gotten greasy; and how their claws turned yellow and cracked and smelled like alligator breath; and how Fluffles didn't smile anymore. And didn't sing. And didn't dance. And didn't do a lot of things they used to do.

They talked about Queen Bagalon; how she treated Emmaline; how she hired the Duke of Dunglewood to kill Pixoratta; how she had, most likely, fed poisoned candy to the Fluffles every night, and how she helped put the dreadful happiness law in place; and how Queen Iliana suddenly disappeared and sailed to Gligoonsburg to become a nun. And they talked about how none of them had ever even heard of a place called Gligoonsburg before.

Mintussus!

EMMALINE, SOFIA, AND PIXORATTA WALKED, or, in Pixoratta's case, hopped, along the side of the pine forest, through the tall grassy plains and over rolling hills with fences and cows and small farms, back towards the castle. They swam when they needed to. They hid when the Queen's guards or greasy Fluffle patrols passed nearby. After several days of walking, swimming, hiding, more walking, and more hiding, they reached the outskirts of town. They hid in a group of trees on a small hill overlooking the castle and watched the townspeople trudge back to their homes and families as the sun set in the sky. They sat on the ridge, watching for several more hours. The skies darkened. Stars twinkled.

"Are you sure you want to do this?" Pixoratta asked the two girls. None of them had slept.

Emmaline looked at Sofia, and Sofia looked at Emmaline. They nodded in agreement. "We're sure," they said.

"And you know a way there?"

"Yes," said Sofia.

"And you still have the piece of candy?"

"Yes," said Emmaline. She patted her pocket, the one Sofia hadn't ripped off.

"Then, I guess it's time for you to go. The sun will come up before too long. You need to make sure you get back before it does. You'll be hard to see at night, but once daylight arrives, the guards will have a much easier time finding you."

"We'll be quick," said Sofia. "You stay here. Get the weight off your leg."

Sofia took Emmaline's hand and they walked towards the town. Crouched really. They'd take a few steps, stop, listen, and take a few more. Emmaline, as best she could, hid behind Sofia's dark fur. They crept behind a house, crawled on their stomachs below the open windows, and rolled under a hedge of bushes next to the street. In the moonlight, the buildings looked ghostly, pale, almost translucent. The candles were out. The fires in the fireplaces were cold; mere embers remained. In a few short hours, sleepy faces would awaken, stoke those embers, and begin their day. But at that moment, the town was dark, except for one building across the street. The fire roared in the ovens and sounds of clinking and clanking could be heard. A sign on the building, hanging loosely from a single hook, had once announced, "DELICIOUS, HOMEMADE BREAD, CAKES, PIES and PASTRY!" but now, broken and bent and missing a large section, it read, "DELICI . . . HOM . . . READ . . . AKES . . . . PI . . . and PAST," as if it didn't want anyone to stop in.

"This is it," said Emmaline. She and Sofia crawled from under the bushes, looked around, saw no one, and raced across the street. They opened the door to the Bakery, cringed as the small bell at the top of the door announced their arrival, and shut the door quickly. The Baker was bent over the oven, putting in a small, sad loaf of black bread.

"A bit early today, aren't you?" she said. She stood up and turned around. "Emmaline! Oh my! I never expected to see you! I thought you were—what are you doing here? You shouldn't be here! The Queen is looking for you. She wants to throw you in jail! Or worse!" She spread her arms wide and hugged Emmaline, stepped back, wiped her hands on her apron, and then hugged her again. The Baker held Emmaline's face in her hands. "Oh, Emmaline! It is so good to see you." She looked down at the small fuzzy creature standing next to Emmaline. "And what is this?"

"This is Sofia. She's my friend. We need your help."

The Baker nodded at Sofia and extended a hand. "A friend of Emmaline's is a friend of mine. Are you . . . are you a Fluffle?" she asked. "You don't look like a Fluffle. You're cute."

"She's a Fluffle. That's what they're supposed to look like," Emmaline said. "But we can't explain right now. We're kinda in a hurry. Can you help us?"

"Oh, Emmaline. I'd be happy to help however I can. What can I do for you? Do you need some food?" The Baker opened and closed several cabinet drawers. "I don't have much—"

"That's OK. We don't need any food, but thank you." Emmaline reached into her pocket, pulled out the green piece of candy, and showed it to the Baker. "We were hoping you could tell us the ingredients in your candy."

The Baker stopped rummaging and said, "Oh, that's not my candy. I don't make those. Queen Bagalon makes them. She said it is a secret recipe and won't share it with anyone."

"Do you think you could try and guess? You're the only person we know who might have an idea." Outside, the sky began to lighten.

"Let me see." She took the candy from Emmaline's hand, and rolled it between her fingers. "It's pretty sticky. I guess some kind of syrup, maybe. I'd say it's made from the sap of a tree or by boiling leaves down. It could be just about anything though. Most of the plants around here are edible. Although, it is *really* green." She held it up to the light from the fire. "I haven't seen anything so green before. And bright green too. Maybe a limelight tree? Or pressed mountain shamrocks? I've never tried them, but either of those would probably make good candy." The Baker sniffed the small piece of candy. "Kind of a minty aroma. . . . Maybe mint. Quite possibly mint, but that's not much of an ingredient for a secret recipe. Mint's in a lot of things."

The Baker held the candy in front of her mouth, stuck out her tongue, and licked the side.

"Eeuuugh! Whath ith that sthuff? Aigh! My tungth's burning! Thath's dithguthting!" She dropped the sticky candy, grabbed her apron, and rubbed her tongue, furiously. It looked like she was trying to scrub off her taste buds. She grabbed a glass of water from a nearby counter and drank the entire thing, before regaining her composure.

"Emmaline, that is horrible! How could anyone eat that?"

"I don't know. Fluffles seem to love it though."

"Hmm. . . ." said the Baker. "I wonder. . . . Come with me." She grabbed a candle, lit it from the fire in the stove, and walked down a hallway towards the back of the building. Emmaline and Sofia followed her.

She turned left through a doorway leading to her library of cookbooks and set the candle down on the table in the center of the room. She scanned the shelves, her finger running along the spines of the books, looking for one in particular. "Where are you? Where are you?" the Baker said, as if the book would answer. "Ah! Here we go!" She put her finger on a book titled *The Complete Guide to Herbs, Spices, and All Forms of Plants, Both Edible and Not-So-Much.* She pulled the dusty book from top shelf, carried it to the table, opened it, and scanned through the pages.

"This little beauty," said the Baker, "was written over two hundred years ago by the great Huliacha, a true magician in the kitchen." The Baker flipped pages. "Mint . . . Mint-of-the-Valley . . . Mintergreen. . . . Ah! Here! Mintussus! Let's see. . . .

The Mintussus is a bright green mushroom that thrives in dark spaces, such as cellars, caves, and dungeons. It is waxy to the touch, and should only be handled with gloves or not at all. Eating the mushroom or juice of the Mintussus is extremely dangerous, as it can cause headaches, confusion, and loss of memory. For other species, especially those in the family Puffus Maximus, such as Puffles, Wuffles, Fluffles, and Cotton-Bellied-Bopples, the Mintussus should be avoided at all costs. The plant causes those species to become progressively more violent, mean, greasy, smelly, and yellow in their eyes and fingertips. It affects their growth and is extremely addictive. Although no known cure exists, some theories suggest that extract of the purple whippleroot might provide relief or possibly an instantaneous cure (since it is biologically the direct opposite of Mintussus). However, this has not been studied in depth. Fortunately, Mintussus has arguably the worst taste in the world, making it very difficult to consume in large quantities.

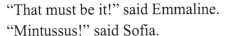

"That must be it!" said Emmaline.

"Mintussus!" said Sofia.

"I would bet my life on it," said the Baker. "That's not a taste I'll soon forget."

"Thank you so much, Madam Baker! C'mon, Sofia! We need to tell Pixoratta!"

"Pixoratta?" said the Baker. "She's gone. How can you—"

"No time to explain!" Emmaline grabbed Sofia's hand and ran to the front door, stopped, opened it a crack, and looked out. The sky was light blue with tips of orange and yellow. The sun had still not made an appearance, but soon would. The town was quiet, although a few lights dotted some of the houses. Emmaline opened the door the rest of the way and started across the street with Sofia. When they reached halfway across the street, the small man with the round glasses stepped out of his house. (To be fair, his glasses were still missing, lost after the Fluffles came to town, so, this morning, he was simply "the small man with no glasses, squinty eyes, and rather poor vision.") His dog, Baxter, sniffed some flowers, then a tree, then a fencepost, before trotting over to Emmaline and sniffing her. Then Baxter sniffed Sofia. The small man with the squinty eyes and rather poor vision turned towards Emmaline and said, "Good morning, Baker! You're out bright and early. And what is this with you? Did you get a dog?" The small man with the

165

squinty eyes and rather poor vision bent over and patted Sofia on the head. "Oh, you're a fluffy one, aren't you? Yes you are! Yes you are! You're so fluffy." He rubbed her ears. "What a cutie! You and Baxter are going to be best friends! I can just tell. Aren't you Baxter?" Baxter looked at the small man with the squinty eyes and the rather poor vision as if he were completely insane, but, to Baxter's credit, did not say so.

Emmaline lowered her voice and mumbled something about having to go get ingredients, then sped off.

"Goodbye, Baker!" said the small man with the squinty eyes and rather poor vision. He waved at the blurry shapes as they ran across the field, up the hill, and to the woods where Pixoratta waited.

"Good morning, neighbor," said the Baker, standing on her front porch. She waved to the small man with the squinty eyes standing in the middle of the road.

"Oh! Good morning again, Baker," he replied. "Back so soon?" He peered at the out-of-focus bushes and blurry door and figure standing alone on the bakery's porch. "Where's your dog?"

Emmaline and Sofia found Pixoratta anxiously anticipating their return. They told her what they had discovered at the Baker's shop. About the how she thought the candy was made from the Mintussus mushroom and how, possibly, the extract of purple whippleroot might, perhaps, be a cure.

"Then I have to go to the Isle of Whipp," said Pixoratta. "The whippleroot grows on the sides of the mountain there. I'll collect it and return tomorrow." She stood up, put a crutch fashioned out of an old tree branch under her arm, and started to head south through the woods.

"Wait. Aren't we going with you?" asked Sofia.

"No. You two need to figure out a way to get the whipperoot to the Fluffles when I get back. It has to be discreet. We need to get the whipperoot to all the Fluffles without being seen. Watch where the guards patrol, when they come and where they go." Pixoratta held Sofia's hands in hers. "You and Emmaline can do anything you set your mind to. You may not know it, but I do." She patted Sofia's long fur. A calmness came over her. "Tomorrow. I'll be back tomorrow."

Pixoratta, with the crutch under her arm, hobbled off through the woods.

Dweezil and Weezil stopped in front of the Baker's shop. They admired their handiwork over the past months, the broken sign out front, the smashed windows, the torn-out railing, the front door which swung crookedly like a drunken man with only one shoe.

"I dare say, Weezil, it's looking to be another fine day." Dweezil grabbed a slat from the picket fence and pulled. The board snapped free, leaving a hole. He walked up to the entrance, patted the board in his hand like a Flibbit player, and whacked the front door with the butt of the wood. It creaked open at an angle.

"Indeed, it is, Boss," said Weezil. "Indeed it is."

Dweezil stepped through the doorway. He and Weezil were the Baker's first customers of the day, every day. Being first meant they got the best bread, or muffins, or sweets, and didn't have to share their loot with anyone.

"Good morning, Baker!" Dweezil sang. His voice grated like two metal forks rubbing together.

"G-good morning, Dweezil," the Baker replied.

"That's *Mister* Dweezil to you!" snapped Weezil.

"Sorry. Yes. Good morning, Mister Dweezil. Mister Weezil." The Baker curtsied. "You surprised me. You're early today."

"Today's bread, if you don't mind."

"Yes, it's not so good today, though," said the Baker.

"Just give us your best loaf."

The Baker went to the oven, pulled out the small, round ball of black bread, and put it on a dishcloth.

"*That* is your best loaf?" said Weezil. "The Queen's not going to like that. It looks like you baked a rock."

"It's the best there is. Really! I haven't had good flour in months."

"Go ahead, blame the flour," said Dweezil. He stepped closer. Then he made a funny expression. His eyebrows pushed together and the end of his nose twitched. He took a step back and pointed his nose in several different directions. "What's that smell?"

"What smell? I don't smell anything," The Baker said. "Maybe the bread?"

Dweezil sniffed, long and hard. "That smell. I recognize that smell . . . it's . . . it's . . ." Dweezil turned and looked at the Baker. All pretense of being nice and charming had fled his expression, not that he had much to begin with. He jumped on top of Weezil's head and pushed his face into hers. "Where is she? "

"W-where is who?"

"The girl."

"W-which girl? There aren't any girls working here."

"Emmaline! I smell her. She was here. Don't you try and hide her."

"Emmaline wasn't here. She ran off. Remember? After the wedding."

"Don't lie to me, Baker! I know she was here."

"No. She's not here," said the Baker. Her voice squeaked like a mouse.

Dweezil swung his pitchfork into a mixing bowl on the counter, smashing it and sending shards flying across the room. His fist shook with fury.

"She had better not be," Dweezil hissed. "If we find out you're harboring a fugitive, you'll spend the next year in the stockade. C'mon Weezil."

Dweezil hopped off Weezil's head. The two Fluffles stormed out of the room, forgetting the bread, and slammed the door behind them, causing it to fall from its hinges. Dweezil kicked the white picket fence on the way past. Slats of wood shattered underneath his foot.

"She was here, Weezil, I tell you. She was here and Sofia was here too."

The Search Begins

QUEEN BAGALON WAS IN A MOST FOUL MOOD. Hearing that Emmaline and Sofia had been in her town, but not caught, was more than she could bear. She paced the throne room, passing from window to window to look out, hoping to catch a glimpse of either Emmaline or Sofia. She dragged her fingernails along the windowsills and etched small grooves into the stone. Bagalon spun from the window and confronted the two Fluffles standing in front of the empty throne.

"The girls, you fools! Emmaline and that blasted Sofia, that's your job!" Bagalon strode over to the throne, past it, and pointed a finger in Dweezil's face. "From now on, you have one job to do!

One! Find Emmaline and Sofia! Find them and deal with them! Capture them if you can, or if you can't, then kill them! Do you understand? Do you think you can do that?"

"We're trying," said Weezil.

"I think—" said Dweezil.

"Trying isn't good enough! And don't think! Catch them! And if you don't catch them, then no more candy! For either of you!"

Dweezil and Weezil stood up straighter.

"Oh, do I finally have your attention? That's right, no more candy unless you bring back Emmaline and Sofia. Do whatever it takes. Get every Fluffle looking for them." She looked at the smelly Fluffles standing in front of her. "What are you waiting for? Go!"

Dweezil and Weezil grabbed their pitchforks and ran out of the room.

Bagalon stood still, thinking for quite some time, and then said, "It's time to change the recipe."

Wanted Posters

DWEEZIL AND WEEZIL STOOD in front of the small man with the round glasses. His shop was a mess—papers scattered everywhere, ink spilled on the counters and floor, broken pencils and paintbrushes. Bits of paper stuck out of his printing press in odd directions, the tables didn't align, the main roller was crooked, and the frame appeared to have suffered through at least one earthquake. Claw marks covered every surface.

"You need a poster, Mr. Dweezil?" he said, speaking directly to Weezil.

"I'm Weezil," said Weezil.

"So sorry. I still haven't found my glasses yet. Makes it very hard for me to see." He turned to the other blurry shape standing in front of him. "And what do you want on the poster, Mr. Dweezil?"

Dweezil looked at the small man with the round glasses, only he still hadn't found his glasses yet, so he was still the small man with the squinty eyes and rather poor vision.

"It needs to say the following: Wanted: dead or alive. Emmaline, a human, and Sofia, a Fluffle. Reward: one hundred golden klonbeks. Both are extremely dangerous and must be captured. They attacked Queen Bagalon and killed the Duke of Dunglewood. If seen, contact Dweezil and

Weezil at once. Anyone offering shelter to the treasonous outlaws will be locked in the dungeon!"

". . . will be locked in the dungeon," said the small man, as he wrote on a pad of paper with a broken pencil. "Heavens! That sounds very harsh!"

"They're *very* dangerous," Weezil hissed.

"By this afternoon, you said?" He looked up at Weezil's blurry shape.

"Yes," said Dweezil. "This afternoon. No later. Put up five hundred copies around town."

"Five hundred copies? That is a lot of copies." Dweezil didn't move or change his expression. "Right. Five hundred copies. I'll get on it."

The small man with the squinty eyes and rather poor vision put the pad of paper down on the edge of a table, too close to the edge, and knocked it onto the floor. He felt around the table for his box of metal letters and begin typesetting. He grabbed a letter *M*, held it next to his nose, squinted, nodded, and put it upside-down in the setting stick. Then he found a lowercase *a*, put it in, then an uppercase *U*, and put it in upside-down and backwards. He then picked up a bent fork, turned it carefully in his hands, said, "Feels like a *T* to me," and put it in the tray next to the *U*. He somehow found a lowercase *e* and *d* and put them in as well, managing to spell out the following:

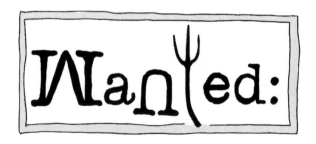

Dweezil exhaled, something between a sigh and a snort, and said, "Oh, for Pete's sake! Here's your glasses." He reached under his left armpit, wiggled his hand around in his fur, and pulled out a pair of round glasses that had been there for several months. "They were sitting right there on the counter. I don't know how you missed them."

"Oh, thank you so much," said the small man with the round glasses—the round, dirty, filthy, greasy, furry, slimy, smelly glasses. (A piece of advice: do not, ever, under any circumstance, store your glasses under a Fluffle's armpit.) The small man put the glasses on his face, blinked twice, took them off, and wiped them on his shirt, leaving a greasy stain. His face lit up with excitement when he put them back on, finally able to see again. Then his smile quickly faded as, for the first time in weeks, he saw the disaster his shop had become.

"Oh my!" said the small man with the round glasses.

"You're welcome." said Dweezil. "And don't forget. If you see Emmaline or Sofia, you tell us."

Cooking in the Dungeon

BAGALON STOOD IN FRONT OF THE WOODEN DOOR in the hallway leading into the dungeons. True to her word, she had not sent a single person to the dungeon since she became Queen. Her feet echoed on the stones and her keys rattled loudly in the door's metal lock. She looked back down the hallway from where she'd come; the hallway was abandoned. She turned the key and opened the wooden door—which swung smoothly on well-worn hinges—and stepped inside.

An eerie green glow illuminated the dungeon hallway. Queen Bagalon's face appeared to smolder in a gray-green light, not unlike the light reflected in a toad's eyes at night. The green appeared to be coming from everywhere and nowhere at the same time. The walls glowed green, and not a healthy green either. It was a green blight, a shimmering sickness, the light of an infection. If you looked at the walls a bit more closely, you would see mushrooms. Thousands and thousands of tiny glowing mushrooms. They covered the walls, floor and ceiling. They shimmered, sometimes bright green, sometimes dark green, and sometimes a range of evil greens somewhere in between. As Queen Bagalon approached, the mushrooms darkened and turned the color of swamp moss. As she passed, and only after she was well past, did they return to their original green.

"These Fluffles are getting to be more trouble than they're worth," Bagalon said to herself. "First Pixoratta starts getting her own ideas, and now the two nincompoops show up."

Queen Bagalon walked into the jail cell through the open door. A table had been placed in the center of the room; several workbenches with beakers and pots and kitchen utensils lined the walls; a large barrel, filled with oily water, sat in the corner. With a grace and smoothness acquired by many of hours of practice, she grabbed a large metal bowl and angrily poured a handful of white grains, something akin to sugar, into the bowl. Then she threw in some brown powder, perhaps cinnamon, perhaps not. She grabbed a knife, hacked a lemon in two, and crushed each half between clenched fists. Juicy pulp dripped through her fingers into the bowl. From a countertop, she picked up a large measuring cup and dunked it into the oily water; then she poured the water into the large metal bowl, and stirred, until the white grains and brown powder and lemon pulp dissolved. She pulled out the spoon, sipped, pondered, added a few more white grains, stirred, sipped again, and nodded her approval. If you had been at your grandmother's house, well, that would have been the end of it. You would have had a nice glass of lemonade to drink, because, of course, your grandmother wouldn't have used oily water from a dirty barrel. However, if you were to taste Bagalon's concoction, you would have tasted some truly awful, extremely oily, lemonade. You would have drunk it or perhaps you would have smiled sweetly while secretly giving it to the cat. But either way you wouldn't have enjoyed it.

But Bagalon wasn't finished.

She took the metal bowl and set it on a small, red granite stone which fit perfectly under the bowl. Then she grabbed a pair of long, heavy leather gloves, something the Blacksmith might use to stoke his fire, or the Baker might use to protect herself while getting muffins out of the oven. Bagalon found a long spatula and scraped some of the gray-green mushrooms from the wall. As soon as the mushrooms separated from the wall, they softened and dripped and oozed. Bagalon held the spatula over the bowl, twisted her hand ever so slowly, and dropped the green slime into the bowl. The water hissed and turned a dark olive. Then the granite under the bowl started to glow red. The bowl turned red and the dark green liquid began to boil. Small bubbles popped on the surface, releasing a yellow-green steam.

The liquid changed color, from dark green to light green to bright green, and thickened, from lemonade, to potato soup, to syrup, and ended as gurgling, bright green, sludge. Bagalon took a large wooden paddle leaning against the barrel of oily water, put it in the water, and stirred it in circles. The surface of the water shimmered as oil spun to the sides. Once the water was spinning quickly, Queen Bagalon grabbed the bowl with the green, bubbling muck, and carefully—oh so carefully—held the bowl over the water and

tipped it. A small drop, a tiny drip of green liquid, fell from the bowl, hit the center of the water, and sizzled. It cooled instantly. A small green candy—a planet spinning in circles of oil—floated on the surface of the water. The spinning water carried it farther and farther from the center until the candy bumped up against the edge of the barrel and was caught in a small metal cage. Bagalon dripped more liquid. Hissing globs of green goop sizzled and spun in the oily black water and turned into candy. Soon, she had emptied the bowl and hundreds of bright green candies filled the cage. She pulled the cage out of the water and poured the candies into a white sack. She took off the heavy leather gloves, tied the sack closed, and said, "There. Let's see how they like a double-dose of mintussus."

The Plan Fails

IT WAS MUCH TOO DANGEROUS for Emmaline and Sofia to walk through the town during the day. If they had been seen by even a single, greasy Fluffle, it would have been all over for them. So, they hid under the bushes at the edge of the field and they planned all night and into the next day.

"If Pixoratta comes back—"

"*When* Pixoratta comes back," whispered Sofia.

"When Pixaratta comes back."

"She'll be back soon, you know. She promised."

"Yes. When Pixoratta comes back," continued Emmaline, "we'll need a way to get all the Fluffles together, to give them the whippleroot. I doubt we can do that. Queen Bagalon has them on patrol, day and night."

Emmaline looked out at the beehive of activity in the town. Wanted posters with her and Sofia's faces dotted every inch of every building. Fluffles poked pitchforks into bales of hay, clumps of flowers, and behind doors, often times poking each other.

"I know! We'll have a party! Not a real party, a pretend party. And when they get there, we'll give them the whippleroot. I'll talk to the small man with the round glasses—he can make up some posters."

"That's not a bad idea, Sofia. We'll put up posters. Come to the party! Get free candy! But instead of mintussis, we'll give them whippleroot and everything will be—" Emmaline stopped. Sofia's fur stood on end.

"Shh! Look!"

At the edge of the field, a small group of soldiers rode next to a pair of large draft horses pulling a wagon. In the back of the wagon, cut, bleeding, dirty, and down-trodden, sat Pixoratta. Her hands were tied behind her back; a large wooden rope held her to the bench. Her head slumped forward. On either side of her were four soldiers, unsmiling and holding swords.

"Pixoratta's been captured!" cried Sofia.

The cart bumped down the path. Pixoratta's head jostled back and forth. Pixoratta glanced up towards their hiding spot in the trees. She suddenly jumped up and thrashed around, biting at the ropes holding her. She got a hand loose, spun, and punched the helmet of the nearest guard. From behind, a guard hit her in the back and knocked her down. Pixoratta's head draped over the side of the cart. She shook wildly, like a wet dog, and a small packet flew out of her fur, fluttered over the side of the cart, and landed in the tall grass next to the road.

Pixoratta turned back and growled. She jumped to the other side of the cart, but by then it was too late. The soldiers grabbed her, held her down, tied her hands twice as tight, and put a burlap bag over her head.

"Did you see that?" exclaimed Emmaline.

"Of course I did! We have to save her!" Sofia leapt from underneath the bushes.

"No! Sit down, Sofia! You'll give away our hiding spot!"

"No one treats the Queen of the Fluffles like that! No one!" she screamed. Sofia ran across the field. The soldiers stared blankly at the tiny puffball racing towards them. Sofia jumped in the cart and attacked the men like a cat caged with a dozen dogs. Her claws flashed. Her teeth gnashed. She snarled and bit and scratched and swung wildly until the hilt of a sword crashed down on her head. Sofia slumped to the floor. Her hands were quickly tied. The men chained her next to Pixoratta in the back of the cart and continued down the path.

Emmaline watched all of it happen, alone at the edge of the woods, helpless to do anything.

"Now what am I going to do?" she said.

The Long Night

The Bakery

EMMALINE WATCHED THE RED SKY DARKEN to violet, then purple. The rolling green hills took on the gray colors of the night. She crawled out from underneath the leaves and bushes, stretched, and let out a small groan. She shook the leaves off her dress. She crept to the road, picked up the small packet that had fallen from Pixoratta's fur, pocketed it, and continued to the town.

Emmaline's first stop was the Bakery.

The Baker, being a baker, had to get up early in the morning and had long since gone to bed. All the lights were out, except for one, a lone candle which burned on a table next to a well-worn chair where the Baker's Husband sat. His head lay against the back of the chair, his hands rested on his belly, and he snored, loudly, like only the husband of a baker can.

Emmaline pushed the bottom of the broken door and slipped inside. She kept her back against the wall, so as not to be seen from the street.

"Pssst! Psst! Wake up!" she said.

The Baker's Husband snored.

"Psst! Psst!"

"ZZZ-zzz-Nnghhnppw- zZZzzZZ . . ."

Emmaline grasped an empty pie pan, and quietly tossed it at the Baker's Husband. It landed on his lap. He sat up with a start, looked down at the empty pan, and mumbled, "Did I eat the whole pie? Oh no! Not again! Honey Bear is going to be so mad."

"Psst! Over here," whispered Emmaline.

The Baker's Husband blinked several times and rubbed his face. He looked around and spotted Emmaline hiding against the wall.

"Over here! It's me, Emmaline."

"Emmaline?" He blinked several more times before waking up all the way. "Emmaline, there are posters up all over the town! The Queen put a one hundred golden klonbek bounty on your head. She's already caught Pixoratta and Sofia. They're in the dungeon and the rumor is they're going be executed tomorrow after the trial. You need to get away as fast as you can, or you'll be next."

"We need to save them. It's not what you think."

Footsteps approached from down the hallway. "What's going on out here?" said the Baker. She rubbed her eyes. A dozen curlers wound around her head.

"We need to save Sofia and Pixoratta!" said Emmaline. "Please, won't you help me?"

"Emmaline, I'll help any way I can. Do you need a place to hide?"

"Thank you. Maybe later, but I have a lot to do before the night is out."

"Well, I'd like to help, but I'm just a baker. I can't break into a dungeon and rescue anyone—or battle my way out for that matter. I'm a lot better in the kitchen than I am anywhere else."

Emmaline pulled the small packet from her dress and held it out.

"What's this?"

"Whippleroot."

"Whippleroot? You don't say." The Baker opened the bag and sniffed the purple flowers inside. "Hmmm. Yes, I daresay it's whippleroot. Fresh too."

"Can you make candy out of it?"

"My wife can make candy out of anything, can't you, Honey Bear?" said the Baker's Husband.

"Well, yes, or at least normally I could. But this is *fresh* whippleroot. It's much too strong for candy. You need to let it dry first. Dried whippleroot, that's something I can work with."

"We don't have time to dry it. I need the candy by tomorrow morning. Isn't there something you can do?"

The Baker took another sniff of the whippleroot.

"I can't promise anything, but I'll see what I can do," she said.

"Oh, thank you so much," said Emmaline. "When you're done, could you please give it to Bella, she'll know what to do with it."

"Bella? The bodybuilder? She doesn't eat candy."

"It's not for her. Just trust me!" Emmaline turned to the Baker's husband. "And you'll need to wear one of your old shirts tomorrow. A big one."

"Why?" said the Baker's husband, as he patted his skinny belly.

"A really big one!" said Emmaline over her shoulder. She ran out of the Bakery off to her next stop.

It was going to be a very long evening for the young girl.

A very, very long evening.

The Dungeon

In the dungeon, chained tightly to the wall, dangled Pixoratta and Sofia. The chains were meant for a person twice their size; their arms stretched out to either side; their feet hung well off the floor. Pixoratta looked miserable. She had been caught just after starting to collect whipploroot plants, and the trip back to the castle had been, to say the very least, brutal. She had been bounced mercilessly in the back of the cart as her captors tormented her.

Sofia only looked slightly better.

"Thank you, Dweezil. Weezil." Queen Bagalon nodded to the two greasy Fluffle goons standing next to her. Their oily fur shimmered an eerie brown-green in the mushroomlight. "You've been very helpful. But now I must talk to our friends, one-on-one. And you need to catch Emmaline before tomorrow's trial. So, if you don't mind, please excuse us." The Queen spoke calmly, as if she were asking the butler to leave her alone to have tea with a good friend and talk about rose gardening. She gave them each a small handful of green candies and ushered them out the door.

Dweezil and Weezil left. The Queen closed the door behind her; she locked it and tucked the key into a hidden pocket deep within the folds of her dress.

"Well, well, well. If it isn't Pixoratta, back from the dead. And her little friend, too, what is your name again? Sarahbelle? Sofullafleas? Sofia! That's it! Sofia." She said the name slowly, drawing out the *e* sound like nails on a chalkboard. "So nice to meet you again, Sofia. Last time I'm afraid I wasn't as charming as I am now. After all, you did ruin my scepter of Tar-Aloon."

Sofia shook against her chains. "I hope you're eaten by a Womba Lizard, you—"

Bagalon's hand shot out and squeezed Sofia's jaw shut. She shook the tiny Fluffle's head and slammed it into the wall. "Hope for all the Womba Lizards you want, you smug little goat, because, come this time tomorrow, you and your friend here will wish a Womba Lizard would kill you!"

Bella's Weight Room

Emmaline stood in Bella's weight room. Tall mirrors covered the walls. *Better to see which muscles need more work*, Bella had explained. Barbells, dumbbells, and all kinds of weights were stacked around the room. They weren't, however, neatly stacked in the weight racks, which had been destroyed by Dweezil and Weezil many months ago. Humungo had promised to build Bella a new set of racks, but hadn't had a chance due to the backlog of Fluffle-sized pitchforks.

"So, you just want me to do is throw it. Is that right?" Bella asked the small girl talking with her.

"Yes. Up to the chandelier. You just need to make sure it gets all the way to the chandelier."

"Up to the chandelier. I think I can do that." She picked up a weight, not too large, about the size of a watermelon, and hefted it in her hands. "Yeah, I can do that."

Emmaline saw a movement reflected in the large mirror across from her. Outside the window, Dweezil and Weezil walked down the street. They stopped, and looked towards Bella's house.

"Oh no!" Emmaline cried, as she dove into a laundry hamper filled with sweaty shirts, dirty towels, and gym clothes.

Dweezil poked his head in the window.

"Who are you talking to, Bella?" He scanned the room.

"What? Oh, no one."

"Now, now. Don't lie, Bella. I distinctly heard you say, 'I think I can do that. Yeah, I can do that.' Who's in there with you?"

"Oh, that? That's just what I say to myself for motivation." She lifted the watermelon-sized weight to her shoulder. "I think I can do that," she grunted. She pushed the weight over her head. "Yeah, I can do that." She lowered the weight. "See? It's just motivation."

"Motivation, huh? How about if we go in there and look around some, Boss? How 'bout that for motivation?"

"Be my guest," said Bella. "There's no one in here but me." She refused to look towards the laundry hamper.

Weezil grabbed the window sill with a claw and pulled himself up. He slid his chest through the window and gasped. "For the love of Nardu, what is that smell?" He fell back out the window, coughing and clutching his nose.

"What smell?" said Bella.

"That stink! It smells like rotten meat and sewage!"

"Oh, that. That's my laundry. After I work out I put my sweaty clothes in the hamper. But there hasn't been any soap lately, so, the clothes just sit there. You're more than welcome to sift through the pile if you want."

"Get on back up there, Weezil! Check the dirty laundry!"

"No way, Boss!" said Weezil, rolling on the ground. "I'm not going near that thing!"

Dweezil thought about it for a second, then turned back to Bella. "You better not be hiding anyone in there."

"No one. I promise. Just me and my weights." She lifted the watermelon-sized weight several more times. "I think I can do that. Yeah, I can do that."

"C'mon, Weezil. We gotta deliver our message anyway. The Queen wants everything done before the trial."

Weezil stood up and the two Fluffles walked away. Bella watched them leave, all the while lifting the watermelon-sized weight and saying, "I think I can do that. Yeah, I can do that." As soon as Dweezil and Weezil turned the corner, Bella looked at the laundry basket and said, "It's OK. You can come out now."

Emmaline burst forth from underneath the sweaty shirts and gasped. "Thank you so much, Bella. You're a lifesaver."

"You're welcome. Now, get out of here, before they come back."

"I will. You're sure you can throw it?"

"Yes. I'm sure."

"All the way to the chandelier?"

"Yes. To the chandelier. Now go!"

Emmaline raced out the door.

"Wait! How will I know *when* to throw it?" Bella asked.

"Don't worry. You'll know!"

Bella stood by the door and watched her leave. The bodybuilder absentmindedly raised and lowered the watermelon-sized weight in her arm. She set it down, and went to close the open window. As she passed the laundry hamper, she stopped, pulled a sweaty shirt out, and held it up to her nose. She took a long sniff and shrugged.

"It's not *that* smelly," she said.

Humungo's Blacksmith Shop

Humungo was not in a good mood. He never liked being woken up at night, especially by the likes of the two greasy Fluffles standing on his bed.

"Rise and shine, sleepyhead!" said Weezil. "Time to get up!"

Dweezil wiggled a sharp toenail in the Blacksmith's left nostril.

"Ugh!" Humungo snorted as he waved a sleepy arm at the smelly Fluffle foot. "Leave me alone."

"Get up!" said Dweezil.

"It's not even midnight. How can it be time to get up?"

"Queen's orders. Get up."

Humungo pulled the blanket up to his face. This time the toenail kicked him.

"Alright! Alright! What does Bagalon want this time?"

"She needs a thousand new pitchforks, by tomorrow morning."

"What on earth could she need a thousand pitchforks for? What's wrong with the pitchforks she already has?"

"Not pretty enough. This is what they need to look like. For after the trial." Dweezil shoved a drawing of an ornate pitchfork into the Blacksmith's large hands. The handle was intricately laced with a braided design similar to a fine rope. Three tines at the end of the pitchfork, resembling the heads of a three-headed serpent, looked extremely sharp.

"Any more questions, Mr. Smarty-pants? No? Good. Get to work."

Humungo sat up and slid his feet onto the cold floor. He grunted, hefted his large frame from the bed, yawned a second time, then walked into his workshop and stoked the fire beneath the forge. He put in a blank piece of metal and heated it until it glowed a hot red, then pulled it out and started to shape it on his anvil. He pounded the metal with a large hammer until it cooled before putting it back in the forge. He did all this without fully opening his eyes.

"Remember, Mr. Smarty-pants, one thousand new pitchforks. By morning."

"Right. One thousand." He yawned, opened his eyes ever so slightly, and caught a glimpse of Emmaline running past his window, which caused his eyes to open wide.

"What was that?" Weezil asked.

"What was what?" said Dweezil.

"That. Over there, Boss. I saw someone run past the window."

"Who was it?"

"I dunno." Weezil jumped on the Blacksmith's anvil and stretched his neck. He peered through the window into the darkness. "I think it was that girl, Emma—ow!" Weezil jumped off the anvil. He held his foot in his hand and hopped around.

"You smashed my toe, you stupid jerk!"

"Oh, sorry about that," said the Blacksmith. "I'm still waking up."

Weezil poked the Blacksmith with a pitchfork.

Dweezil raced out the door. "C'mon, Weezil! Let's go catch her!" Weezil hopped behind.

The Blacksmith put the finished pitchfork to the side, and grabbed the first of nine-hundred-ninety-nine more pitchforks he had to make before the night was over.

Oh, that poor girl. At least I slowed him down for you, he thought.

Back in the Dungeon

In the dungeon, Queen Bagalon plucked a green candy from the oily water and waved it in front of Pixoratta's sagging head.

"I bet you're hungry. It looks good, doesn't it?"

Pixoratta's eyes opened. She stared at the small piece of candy in front of her, tracking its movement like a hypnotist's watch.

"Yes. You want it, don't you? You want the candy."

Pixoratta moved her head from side to side. "No."

"Really? No candy for you?"

Pixoratta shook her head again, but not as far. She hung from the chains, her head drooped. She opened her mouth.

"NO!" Sofia screamed. "Don't eat it! Don't do it! It's poison!" Sofia's fur stood on end. She struggled against the chains.

Time seemed to slow as Sofia watched Queen Bagalon reach forward and place the candy on Pixoratta's tongue. The Fluffle Queen closed her mouth, sucked the candy, and smiled.

"Yes. It's good, isn't it? So good. . . . That's a good girl. Eat it up. How about another? Maybe one more?"

Pixoratta nodded.

Davinda's House

Emmaline ducked into Davinda's house. She closed the door behind her and held her breath as first Dweezil ran, then Weezil hopped, past the doorway.

"Emmaline? But, I thought you were captured," said the sleepy Davinda.

"No, they captured Sofia and Pixoratta, but not me."

"You need to hide. I could try to hide you here. They said they'll arrest anyone who even thinks about helping you, but I'm willing to try."

Emmaline took a breath and continued. "I don't need you to hide me, but I do need your help. I need your trapeze skills."

"What? My trapeze skills?"

"Yes. Tomorrow."

"Tomorrow? Emmaline, what are you talking about?"

"Do you remember the routine you did last year, at Queen Iliana's birthday party?"

"Sure. It was the first time anyone had done a quadruple somersault."

"Yes, but I don't need you to do that. I just need the first part, when your partner threw you in the air and caught you."

"That? Oh, that's easy. You should ask for something more challenging."

"Only *I* need to *be* your partner, and I need you to *not* catch me."

"*Not* catch you? I said *challenging*, not *deadly*, Emmaline."

"Just trust me. Can you do it?"

"I guess so. I'm not used to *not* catching someone in the air, but I'll try."

"Oh thank you! Thank you so much!"

"You're welcome. I guess. Wait. Why do you want me to not catch you?"

"No time to talk! You'll see tomorrow!"

Emmaline went to leave, but Davinda quickly pushed her behind the front door. She looked outside.

"Uh oh! Here come Dweezil and Weezil! Quick! Out the back!"

Emmaline scampered to the back of the house, where Davinda's practice trapeze and diving boards and trampolines filled the yard. She ran behind several houses and down a side street.

"Davinda. Davinda. Davinda." Dweezil walked up the steps and onto the trapeze artist's front porch. He held out his hands in a warm greeting, as if he were getting ready to hug a long-lost friend.

"What do you want, Dweezil?"

"Really? No hug for me? No hug for your buddy, Dweezil?" He waited for a hug that wasn't coming then put his arms down. Weezil hopped one-footed up the steps behind him.

"We're looking for the girl, Emmaline. And, I think I just heard her behind that door, so if you don't mind. . . . Aha!" He jumped past Davinda, ready to grab a small girl hiding behind the door.

But there was no small girl hiding behind the door.

"I was just heading off to bed," said Davinda. "Divers and trapeze artists need their rest and have to go to bed early, and since I'm both, I need to go to bed twice as early. So, if you don't mind . . ." She pushed Dweezil out the door.

Dweezil said, "Something smells fishy to me."

"Kinda like dirty laundry," added Weezil before they resumed their search for Emmaline.

The Jeweler's

Emmaline's next stop was the Jeweler's.

She hid under the large workbench in the corner of the room and whispered up to the Jeweler.

"Does it spin?" Emmaline said.

"Well, no, of course not. I mean, they used to, all my chandeliers used to spin, but when that one fell on the cake, I had to reinforce them. I put in a special locking pin to keep them from rotating."

"And what if someone took out the locking pin? Then would it spin?"

"Well, yes, but you need a special key to take out the locking pin."

"Could I borrow it?"

"The special key?"

"Yes."

"Well, certainly, if you need it to rescue Pixoratta and Sofia, I guess so. It's back in my supply closet. Let me go get it for you." The Jeweler walked to the back of the room, down a small hall, opened a door, and stepped into a large closet filled with metal bits and gems and jewelry and tools and everything a Jeweler could ever need.

The Jeweler's front door opened.

Dweezil and Weezil crept in. They tiptoed around the jewelry cases, searching. They opened drawers and looked inside.

"I found it!" shouted the Jeweler from the closet, "Although I really have no idea how loosening one of my locking pins could save Pixoratta and Sofia. It seems—" She jumped as she faced Dweezil and Weezil at the end of the hall. Behind them, unseen by either Fluffle, Emmaline cowered under a workbench. Her eyes were wide. Her body, motionless.

"You found something, did you, Jeweler?" said Dweezil.

"Um. Good evening, gentlemen," the Jeweler replied. She put her hands behind her back with the special unlocking key and pressed up against the wall.

"Funny, we happen to be looking for something, too," said Dweezil.

"Maybe you've heard of it," said Weezil. "It's called an 'Emmaline'. It has brown hair, a white dress, is skinny, and wanted for murder. Ever seen anything like that?"

"No. Never," said the Jeweler.

"Maybe you have one hiding back in your supply room, huh?"

"Seems like a good place to store an Emmaline if you ask me, Boss."

Dweezil pushed past the Jeweler and stuck his head in the supply room.

"No. No one's in there," said the Jeweler. Weezil hopped forward to check. The Jeweler moved out of his way, side-stepping towards the workbench with the crouching girl underneath it. Dweezil and Weezil stood in the supply room. The Jeweler heard them knock over a few jars, pocket a few gems, and poke the walls.

"Any secret doors in here, Jeweler? Seems like a good place to have a secret door. Maybe a hidden room, too."

The Jeweler slid sideways and stood in front of the workbench. She fluffed her dress out as wide as it would go, much wider than Emmaline's small body, and leaned against the workbench.

Dweezil poked his head out of the supply room and back into the hallway. "No? Really? No hidden doors?" Weezil poked his head out next to Dweezil's. "Maybe a trapdoor?"

"No. No hidden doors. N-no trapdoors either," she stammered. "Why would you think Emmaline is here? She's been missing for a week or more. I haven't seen her."

Dweezil smiled and his sharp teeth peered out from under his lips. "Well, Weezil and I were just walking around, when we noticed footprints in front of your shop. Muddy footprints, the kind of footprints made from running through the dirt next to the trampoline behind Davinda's house, for example."

Emmaline looked down at her feet. Mud caked them from top to bottom. She grimaced.

"So, we thought, maybe you had a visitor." He looked around the room, then stepped closer to the Jeweler. He pressed his face up against hers as she leaned farther back, her dress fluffed wide, helping to hide Emmaline under the workbench. His breath smelled like lizards.

"No. No visitors. The only one to go in and out is Mr. Pickles." She looked at the shelf above the workbench. There was Mr. Pickles, half-asleep, in his favorite spot. "But he's right here. Aren't you, Mr. Pickles?"

Mr. Pickles purred.

"You really think I can't tell the difference between *human* footprints and *cat* footprints?" said Dweezil. "You're out of your mind! And you must be crazy if you think I don't know someone's hiding under that workbench."

"*This* workbench? No, haha! No one is hiding under *this* workbench," the Jeweler said. She grabbed the top of the workbench with her hands. Her knuckles turned white.

"Don't lie to me. That workbench. I can smell her. Now move aside."

"Let me move her, Boss." Weezil pointed his pitchfork at the Jeweler.

The Jeweler laughed, a nervous little laugh, and scooted a step to the left. Emmaline crawled sideways, keeping the Jeweler's dress between her and Dweezil.

"All the way," said Dweezil.

The Jeweler slid two more steps sideways. She tapped Emmaline on the head and opened a hand, exposing the special key she had retrieved from the supply room. Emmaline took the key and placed it in a pocket.

"You wanna poke?" Weezil shook his pitchfork.

"No. No. No. No pokes." The Jeweler held up her hands, empty palms facing outward, and slid the final step sideways.

Dweezil smiled at her, nodded, and started to bend down to pull out Emmaline from under the table. At the exact same time, Mr. Pickles (who didn't like to be more than two steps from his owner), stood up, arched his back, took two steps

sideways, knocked over a jar, and spilled iridescent powder everywhere. A shiny cloud of dust sparkled from the sky.

"What—" Dweezil and Weezil said in unison. They looked up, just at the exact moment the shiny metal flakes fell like sticky snow. The Jeweler paused, for the merest second, then swirled her dress away from the workbench, creating a swoosh of air that blew the sparkling flakes all over the grimy Fluffles' faces.

"Aigh! My eyes! I can't see!" shouted Dweezil. Weezil brushed at his face, trying to push the powder from his eyes.

Emmaline saw the two Fluffles clawing at their faces. She saw the open door to the workshop, which led to the main room, and through the main room, she saw the open door to the outside.

"Oh! My heavens! You poor things!" the Jeweler cried. "Here, let me help you get that out of your eyes." She put one hand on Weezil's face and rubbed side to side, mashing sparkling powder deeper into his eyes. With the other hand, she grabbed the half-full bottle of iridescent powder and furiously shook the remainder of the bottle over their heads; a cloud of shiny metal powder filled the air around them. She reached down, pulled Emmaline out from under the counter, gave her a knowing look, and pushed the girl towards the door.

"Oh my! It looks like you got some more in your eyes!" she said as she pushed the pile of powder on top of Dweezil's head over his eyes. "Let me get that for you."

"Stop helping me, you fool!" shouted Dweezil. He pushed the Jeweler away from him.

The Jeweler grabbed a sheet of metal from the workbench next to her. "Oh, careful! Watch out! You're going to walk into that wall." The Jeweler bashed the metal on Weezil's face. He fell over and crashed on the floor.

Emmaline raced on tiptoe through the room, through the workshop, and through the doorway outside. All the while, a cloud of sparkly dust blinded—and the Jeweler bashed—the two Fluffle hooligans.

Dweezil spun frantically and waved his arms. "Don't touch me!"

"Oh, sorry, I was just trying to help. You have a little spot over there," said the Jeweler. She brushed his shoulder to no avail.

"Stop touching me!" Dweezil smacked away her hand.

Dweezil and Weezil stopped flailing about. Weezil's entire face was covered with shiny powder. He blinked his eyes. They looked like two yellow orbs in the center of a greasy, furry rainbow.

Dweezil brushed furiously, but the powder clung to his oily fur. He shook like a wet dog covered in sparkly glue.

The powder didn't move.

"Aigh! How do you get this stuff off?" Dweezil shrieked.

"Ah, yes. Well, see, that's my special, *iridescent* powder. You have to pick it up a single flake at a time. Otherwise, it just sticks to whatever it touches."

"Are you nuts? I have to pick this out a single flake at a time? It would take years!"

"Well, it is meant to last. It wouldn't work if it flaked off the jewelry. Washing it won't work either. Your best bet is to shave your fur off," said the Jeweler.

"We're not shaving our fur, you dundersnoot!"

Dweezil grunted, glared under the workbench, saw it was empty, and smashed a lamp sitting by the window. "C'mon Weezil. Let's get outta here."

The two Fluffles marched out of the store like a pair of grouchy rainbow trout.

"So sorry you didn't find what you were looking for! Come back again soon!" The Jeweler waved at their shimmering backs as they stomped towards the castle.

She sighed, then said, "That was worth it, Mr. Pickles, but now I have to clean up the mess." She turned back to the workbench and found not a single grain of powder had fallen on the floor, or the workbench, or anywhere other than on Dweezil and Weezil's sticky fur.

"Well, would you look at that? Not a drop anywhere. Nicely done, Mr. Pickles. I am *so happy* you spilled that bottle of iridescent powder!"

Mr. Pickles stretched, swished his tail once, and fell back asleep.

Back to the Dungeon

Pixoratta dropped her head. She hung from the dungeon wall like a dying octopus. Every so often her shoulder would twitch, or her head would shake, but for the most part, she simply dangled between two chains. Her belly was swollen and green spittle dripped from her mouth.

Bagalon stood back and looked at the over-stuffed Fluffle queen before turning her attention to the small Fluffle chained next to her. Sofia looked fierce, or as fierce as possible, considering she was chained to a wall in a dungeon and had just witnessed her dear queen eat several hundred poisonous green candies.

"You're a monster, Bagalon! An evil, horrible monster!"

"Ha ha! How cute!" Bagalon patted Sofia on the top of the head like a little child. "No, I wouldn't say I am a monster. But I do know what I like, and I also know what I *don't* like. And right now I don't like the thought of you and Pixoratta stirring up any more trouble."

Bagalon looked in the barrel, but only saw her reflection in the black, oily water.

"Well, how about that? We're all out of candies and I don't have time to make more. It looks like it must be your lucky day."

Sofia made the mistake of relaxing, just a bit.

Bagalon continued. "I'm sure we can manage something." She pulled on her heavy leather gloves, took the spatula, and scraped a large blob of glowing mintussus mushrooms from the wall. She put the goop-covered spatula up to Sophia's mouth like she was feeding a baby. "Here you go. Be a good girl. Take a big bite now."

Sofia bit the edge of the spatula and shook her head, ripping the spatula out of Bagalon's hand and spitting it to the floor.

"Oh, Sofia! That was a mistake. A very *big* mistake. I guess we can do this the hard way. In a way, I kind of prefer it."

Bagalon sliced off another section of mushrooms and walked back to Sofia. She stood there, in front of her captive, quiet. Sofia clenched her jaws together. They stared at each other, not saying anything. Sofia's eyes burned. Her nostrils flared. Bagalon smiled sweetly, sighed, and then punched Sofia in the stomach. Hard. Really hard. All the air whooshed out of Sofia's lungs. As she opened her mouth to gasp for a breath, Bagalon shoved the green, oozing mushrooms into Sofia's face and slapped a crushing hand over the poor Fluffle's mouth. Her hand was an iron lock. Sofia gulped for air, couldn't get any, and swallowed. The mushrooms burned her mouth and throat as they slid down into her stomach.

Sofia gagged and coughed.

Mushrooms came out her nose.

And then she didn't feel so well. Or maybe she felt really well. She wasn't sure. It was a feeling she had never felt before—one of complete relaxation coupled with an intense desire to throw up. She stopped fighting.

"That's better. Let me get you a little more." Bagalon cut off another section of mushrooms with the spatula, this time directly into her gloved hand. She squashed mushrooms in Sofia's mouth, up her nose, and down her throat. Sticky green glowing goo was everywhere. "How about a little more?" Bagalon grabbed more mintussus, shoved it in Sofia's mouth, and asked, yet again, "How about a little more? Yes?"

This horrific scene repeated itself, over and over, until Bagalon's face glistened with sweat.

Finally, Bagalon stopped.

Sofia, covered in glowing mintussus goop, hung from the chains. Her lungs barely moved. Her head fell forward and her tongue, green and swollen, dangled from her mouth.

Back to Humungo's

The sun was beginning to rise in the sky. Emmaline's final stop was Humungo's house. Although it was still nighttime, she walked in to find the Blacksmith hard at work.

"There! One thousand!" he said to the closing door. "One thousand bright and shiny new pitchforks for the Queen. I hope you're happy! Now I'm going back to bed—Oh! Emmaline! I thought you were Dweezil coming to collect these blasted pitchforks."

"No, it's just me."

"Are you OK? You look tired. Have you been up all night?"

"I'm fine," she sighed. "I need your help though."

"My help with what?"

"I need you to pull a rope at the trial."

"I'm not pulling on any gallows noose, if that's what you're asking. I won't have anything to do with any hanging. No matter how much I want to see those Fluffles punished. No ma'am! Not me!"

"No, no. I just need you to pull a rope, as hard as you can," Emmaline assured him. "I'll throw it to you and you pull it."

"Sure. I can pull a rope. But why?"

"Because you're the strongest person in town."

"What about Bella, the bodybuilder? She's stronger than me."

"OK, you're the *second* strongest person in town. But she's going to be busy with another job. Will you do it?"

"Of course I'll do it. How will I find you? I don't suppose you're going to just walk in there? Bagalon would arrest you in a second. Less than a second."

"No, I'm not going to just walk in there. But don't worry. You won't have a problem finding me. I guarantee it."

"Ok. I'll pull a rope, at the trial, just for you. I promise."

"Oh, and Humungo, could you do one more thing for me?"

"What's that, Emmaline?"

"Could you maybe make those pitchforks not so sharp?"

Back to the Baker's

Emmaline snuck through the town. The sun was just barely touching the bottom of the horizon when she arrived back at the Bakery. The Baker scurried and led Emmaline into a dark storage pantry, where she closed the door all but a crack and promised to return in a few hours. Emmaline lay down on a large bag of flour.

She stared at the ceiling.

Emotions raced through her body like lightning.

She couldn't possibly fall asleep.

And then she fell fast asleep.

The Dungeon (Yet Again)

In the dungeon, Queen Bagalon washed the mashed green mintussus from her dress. She whistled absentmindedly, something you might do while walking down a country road on a sunny day without a care in the world.

Dweezil and Weezil slunk down the dungeon hallway, sparkling as if they had been thrown up on by an ill Glitteroponus.

"What?" shouted Queen Bagalon. "What happened to you? Why are you so . . . so . . . SPARKLY?"

"Tell her, Boss," said Weezil.

"Mr. Pickles attacked us," said Dweezil.

Queen Bagalon scrunched up her face, as if she were trying to suck a watermelon through a straw.

"You see, we were at the Jeweler's store—"

"Wait! You mean you were attacked by Mr. Pickles, *the cat?*"

"He attacked out of nowhere! We were—"

"I don't want to know! Don't even tell me! Did you find the girl? That's all that matters. Did you find that bratty child, Emmaline?"

"Well, um . . . no."

"You fools! How could you not find her? She's around here somewhere! Argh! I'm surrounded by idiots!"

Dweezil and Weezil shuffled uncomfortably on their feet.

"What to do? What to do?" the Queen thought out loud. "Never mind. It's too late to catch her. Just keep an eye out for her at the trial. She'll probably try something sneaky to save her precious little friends. And for Pete's sake, get rid of that stupid powder! You look ridiculous!"

"Well, you see, um, you can only pick it off a single flake at a time, so it's, um really hard to—"

"We have an execution in two hours! Two executions! Do whatever it takes to get that off your body or I'll execute the two of you as well!"

Queen Bagalon rubbed her forehead. She, like Emmaline and so many townspeople, had had a very long night.

The Trial

THE SUN CAME UP. The birds sang. It was another beautiful day—if you didn't notice the broken buildings and shattered windows and cracked fences. It also helped if you didn't notice the posters plastered throughout the town, offering a one hundred golden klonbek reward for the capture of the kingdom's most heinous criminal, Emmaline. And, even more than that, if you didn't hear the trumpets and the blaring announcement that, in a mere fifteen minutes, the trial of Pixoratta and Sofia—murderous felons!—would begin. And the trial would end, shortly thereafter, with their execution. If you didn't notice any of those, it would have been the most wonderful day to sleep in, or go fishing, or sit under a tree and read a good book about cleaning an old man's garage. But, if you did happen to notice any of those (and of course you did), you would find it was a rather bleak and dreary day, regardless of what the sun was saying.

Inside the castle's Great Hall, row after row of benches faced the main platform. In the center, a red curtain draped over a large box the size of a small room. It was hard to tell what was inside the box. It resembled a magician's cage, and perhaps held a ferocious tiger, or soon-to-be-vanished assistant, or both, but probably not, because of the snoring. Terrifying *snorts* and *snoots* emanated from the curtain-covered box. The kind of snoring that woke baby dragons at night. A throne sat behind a small desk a short distance from the snoring cage. On the desk lay a wooden gavel, a pen, and a small book. Otherwise, the Great Hall was empty.

Upstairs, Queen Bagalon, sat in front of her looking glass and prepared for the trial of Pixoratta and Sofia. She had bathed, cleaned the bits of mushroom out of her hair, and now stuck her lips out, not unlike a camel, to put on crimson lipstick. Her servants brushed her hair, and, when that was done, placed a delicate crown on her head. She whistled and smiled and looked positively angelic.

Outside, townspeople marched in groups of twos and threes, sometimes fours or fives, towards the castle; they formed lines near the castle gate, flowed through the two doors into the Great Hall, and took their seats on the waiting benches.

In the bakery, the Baker opened the door to the storage pantry. A shaft of light snuck through the doorway and illuminated Emmaline's sleeping body. Worn out and exhausted, Emmaline had fallen instantly asleep and hadn't moved since. The Baker bent down and brushed a hair from Emmaline's face.

"Emmaline, dear, time to wake up," she said.

Emmaline stretched, and slowly woke. She looked around, confused. It took her a moment to remember she was in the Baker's storage room, sleeping on a bag of flour.

"Did you sleep well?"

Emmaline blinked her eyes before answering. "I think so. I don't even remember falling asleep."

"Are you sure you want to do this? You could still run away. Now would be a perfect time. Everyone will be at the trial."

"No. I can't abandon my friends. I have to do this. *We* have to do this."

"You're very brave, Emmaline."

The Baker's lips smiled, but her eyes were sad. She opened the door the rest of the way.

The Baker's Husband entered the room. He wore a white shirt, ten or twelve sizes too large. It billowed around his frame like ship's sail.

"Well, then Emmaline, I guess it's time to climb in," he said as he raised the bottom of his shirt.

Several minutes later, the Baker and her husband joined the groups of twos and threes, sometimes fours or fives, and walked towards the castle. The Baker walked, but the Baker's Husband wobbled and tottered. He struggled and lurched from side to side. Two greasy Fluffles, sitting on a stone wall with a wanted poster of Emmaline plastered on the rocks under their feet, took note. They hopped off the wall and walked after the Baker and her husband.

"Hey! What'd you do, fat man? Eat a chocolate-glazed elephant last night?"

"You were so skinny yesterday and now you're fat again. Look at all those fat lumps under your shirt!"

The Baker slid a hand into her husband's and squeezed. He smiled—just the corners of his mouth—and teetered forward. A bead of sweat dripped down his forehead. The Fluffles were wrong about him being fat—he was no fatter than he had been ten minutes earlier. What they didn't realize was what they thought was a half-digested, chocolate-glazed elephant was actually Emmaline, hidden under the Baker's Husband's oversized shirt. His belly lumps were her elbows and knees, feet and head, poking his shirt in odd ways.

"Look at that! He's so fat, he has to grab his belly to keep it from falling out of his shirt!"

The two Fluffles laughed and slapped their own bellies. The Baker forced a smile and then she and her husband shuffled forward. A few of the townspeople noticed how fat he had gotten overnight, *like a ripe cantaloupe* one thought, but no one said anything. The Baker sat in the very center of the Great Hall, underneath the largest chandelier. Her lumpy husband shuffled over and sat next to her.

More and more townspeople squeezed in and filled the benches. The Jeweler fidgeted with a small clasp on her bracelet. Humungo sat next to the small man with the round glasses. Davinda sat in the balcony, near the trapeze from last year's party. Hushed conversations flitted about the room; mostly about Pixoratta, Sofia, and the snoring coming from under the red curtain.

Trumpets blared. The sound of claws on stone pounded like rusty drums as Fluffles swarmed into the room. They surrounded the benches of townspeople. Each Fluffle held a new pitchfork, made the night before, and pointed it inwards, towards the center of the room. They looked like there was nothing they'd rather do than use their new weapons.

Queen Bagalon appeared at the top of the Grand Staircase. She radiated beauty and happiness. She smiled and waved to her subjects, who did not wave back. She descended the staircase, her long dress flowing behind her, and sat in the waiting throne. Behind her—looking much less beautiful and radiating absurdity, embarrassment, and ridiculousness—appeared Dweezil and Weezil. Overnight, they'd had a transformation which eclipsed even the Baker's Husband's sudden weight gain. They looked, quite frankly, stupendously silly.

(It is here I have to tell a side story. As you recall, Dweezil and Weezil hadn't found Emmaline, but were instead covered in iridescent powder thanks to Mr. Pickles the cat. *Get rid of that stupid powder!* Queen Bagalon had cried; and they tried. They scrubbed with soap, disgusting as that was to the Fluffles. They picked at each flake with useless claws. They chewed the gum of a goobluk tree, spat it into their hands, and pressed it into each other's fur, hoping it would stick to the powder. It didn't. The goobluk gum instead stuck to their fur and only added to the problem. Dweezil and Weezil scrubbed vinegar into their fur to dissolve the gum and waited, but nothing happened. *Freezing the gum might work*, they thought with the notion that once frozen they could snap the gum out of their fur. So they filled a large vat with ice cubes, added water, and sat in the cold bath until their lips turned blue and their skinny arms shook. But the gum, and the iridescent flakes, refused to let go. And so, stinking of goobluk gum and vinegar, shaking uncontrollably from nearly freezing to death, and shining like two oil slicks in a sewer, they did the only thing they could: they shaved each other's fur off. You might expect you would get a bad haircut from a shivering, smelly Fluffle whose claws weren't made to hold scissors, and you'd be right. They hacked away at each other with the scissors. Clumps of fur fell to the ground, exposing their pink skin underneath. They chopped, sometimes too much, sometimes way too much. Sometimes they chopped something that didn't need to be chopped at all, like an eyebrow. They looked, in a word, absurd. And that is how they appeared at the top of the stairs.)

Queen Bagalon banged the gavel and demanded order, even though the room hadn't been particularly noisy. The few hushed conversations stopped.

"Ladies and Gentlemen, today we have the unfortunate obligation to hold a trial to determine the guilt of Pixoratta and Sofia, who have been charged with the death of the Duke of Dunglewood. Dweezil and Weezil, please bring in the accused!" She looked behind her and saw Dweezil and Weezil with their new haircuts. She snapped her head back, raised her eyebrows, and glared at the Fluffle henchmen. But she did not say anything.

Dweezil and Weezil stepped to the red velvet curtain, and, with a grand flourish, pulled it off the cage. An audible, collective gasp came from the assembled townspeople. Inside the cage, as if relaxing in a zoo, two creatures slept. Both snored loudly and neither remotely looked like a Fluffle anymore. Maybe a sopping-wet cat, but not a Fluffle. Their claws were dark green, split and cracked. Black oily fur clung to their bodies. Green-black drool dribbled from their mouths and merged with crusty slime around their lower jaws and bellies. They bore no resemblance to Pixoratta and Sofia, other than one being smaller than the other, and one wearing a crown, whereas the other did not.

"C'mon! Wake up, sleepyheads!" Dweezil and Weezil poked the two prisoners through the cage. Sofia groaned, belched up a gob of green goo, which dribbled down her chin. She stared at the far wall and made no attempt to wipe the goo from her face, even after it began to slide down the front of her neck. Pixoratta groaned and moved slowly.

Bagalon waved an arm. "Yes, well, let us begin, shall we? Pixoratta and Sofia, you have been accused of the murder and subsequent dismemberment of the Duke of Dunglewood in the Swamps of Smugnuk by swampworms. How do you plead?"

Pixoratta shook her head slowly, as if she were trying to think but couldn't remember how. She blinked her eyes, examined the cage, looked past the bars, and saw the crowd

of townspeople surrounded by Fluffles with pitchforks. She turned her head towards Queen Bagalon. When the Queen's face came into view, Pixoratta exploded with fury. She flew against the bars. Queen Bagalon backed away in her chair, even though the cage's heavy metal bars were safely between them. Pixoratta's claws scratched at the metal and swung harmlessly towards Queen Bagalon.

"BLAAARGH! BLAAK BLAAARGH! KARG SCHMA-GA-GARG!!" Pixoratta screamed. Green spittle flew from her mouth with each word.

"I'm sorry? What's that?" Queen Bagalon replied. She had regained her composure and sat, haughtily, in her throne behind the small desk.

"BLEAAAUUUG!! BLEEEUG!! BLARG MAA-GARD!!" Pixoratta replied as she shook the bars. Green froth bubbled from her mouth.

"Yes. Well. Indeed. Not sure what that means, so I will just put down the defendant pleads guilty," said Bagalon, which was met with more cage-rattling, spittle-flinging, and incoherent screaming from Pixoratta.

"Duly noted. And what about the other defendant? Sofia, how do you plead?"

Sofia stared at the far wall. The gob of green mucus slid farther down her belly, leaving a trail behind it like a slug.

"No? Nothing? Does the defendant wish to answer? No? I'll just do it for you then. G-U-I-L-T-Y. Guilty." She jotted the plea into the book, dotting the *i* in guilty with firm flick of her wrist, then snapped the book shut. "Now, let's see, what's next? Oh yes, we need punish the criminals. Dweezil, what is their punishment?"

"Death," he replied.

"Oh yes, that's right. Death! Such a shame, but unless anyone has any objections, I guess—"

"I OBJECT!" screamed a small voice from the center of the large room.

Fluffle Popcorn

"What? Who said that? Who dares object to my decision?" Queen Bagalon searched the great room.

"I OBJECT! Pixoratta and Sofia are innocent! You WILL NOT execute my friends!" Emmaline stood on the bench between the Baker and her husband. She had wiggled loose from under the Baker's husband's shirt and listened to the trial, hoping against hope that somehow her friends would be found innocent.

"Emmaline! What a pleasant surprise," smiled Queen Bagalon. She tented her fingers together in front of her chest. "And here I thought we'd have to track you down."

Dweezil and Weezil grabbed their pitchforks tighter and took a step towards the small girl.

"Bagalon, you WILL NOT execute my friends!" Emmaline's fists were braced against her hips.

"Oh, you are precious, you silly girl. I'm the Queen, and I get to execute whoever I want. Who's going to stop me?"

"I am! And everyone here! The townspeople will! We'll all stop you!"

"Just like you saved Queen Iliana?"

A hush fell over the room.

"Oh, don't be stupid! Do you really think she went to Gligoonsburg to become a nun? Honestly! I killed her! Locked her in a cave! And there's nothing you can do about it! I'm the Queen and I have an *entire army* of Fluffles! Look around you! You're surrounded! And they'd do anything for some candy, wouldn't you?" Bagalon looked at the Fluffles surrounding the townspeople. They *clanged* their pitchforks against the floor.

Queen Bagalon wiggled her fingers in a slight wave. "Dweezil! Weezil! Get her!"

Dweezil and Weezil jumped and ran towards Emmaline. They leapt from the front of the platform; they crawled over the heads and arms and shoulders of the townspeople.

Emmaline turned to the back of the room. She raised both her arms over her head and spread her fingers wide. "Now, Davinda! Now!"

From the balcony, Davinda grabbed the trapeze bar and swung over the edge. She looped her knees over the bar and hung, upside down, as she swung forward. She grabbed Emmaline by both wrists and *swooshed* forward, over Dweezil and Weezil's heads. Up, higher and higher they swung, until, at the last minute, Davinda let go. Emmaline sailed through the air. She spun several times, and landed on the large chandelier, high in the air in the middle of the room. She grabbed the fixture tightly, took out the special key the Jeweler had made for her, and quickly released the locking nut. The chandelier started to wobble and spin on its chain.

Queen Bagalon stared at Emmaline hanging onto the chandelier. She had been caught off guard, but she didn't stay that way for long. "Get her, you fools!" she cried. "Don't let her get away!"

Emmaline unwound a rope from her waist and wrapped a large section around the chandelier's chain as fast as she could. She knotted one end of the rope to one of the chandelier's arms.

Fluffles threw their pitchforks at Emmaline. The sharp points flew past her face and chunked into the wooden beam above her head.

Emmaline shouted down to the benches far below. "Bella! The bag! Throw me the bag!"

Bella held a watermelon-sized bag in her hand. It was white, lumpy, tied shut with a cord, and, written on the side, were the words "Property of LuLu's Bake Shop." She threw the bag in the air. It sped upwards. Emmaline, sitting on the chandelier, caught the bag as more pitchforks whizzed past. She tore the cord off the top of the bag, then threw down the long end of the rope to Humungo. "PULL!" she yelled.

Humungo grabbed the end of the rope. The massive blacksmith, with arms like tree trunks, pulled, harder than anyone had ever pulled a rope before. And as he pulled the rope, the chandelier started to unwind and spin in circles like a merry-go-round. Faster and faster it spun. The room circled under Emmaline's feet, but she did not let go. Whirling in circles on the spinning chandelier, she yelled, "WHOOO WAAAANTS CAAAAAANNNDDDYY?"

The Fluffles froze. They stared towards the sky. They stopped throwing pitchforks. "CANDY! CANDY! CANDY!" they shouted.

Emmaline tilted the bag downwards, and out poured hundreds of purple candies. Only they didn't pour straight down, since she was pouring them from a quickly spinning chandelier. Instead, the purple candies flew far and wide, across the entire room. Purple candies rained from the sky. Fluffles dropped their pitchforks, and jumped after the candy. They climbed on top of each other. Over each other. As they popped purple candy between their lips their mouths were filled with the sweet taste of whipperoot. And it was delicious. They *mmm'd* and *oooh'd*. They sat and sucked on

the Baker's whipperoot candy. They dropped any remaining pitchforks on the floor next to them. They lay back and savored the sweet taste, letting it wash their mouths of mintussus. The commotion in the room stopped. The only sound was the slowing squeak and click of the spinning chandelier.

Queen Bagalon surveyed the room. A thousand Fluffles relaxed around a circle of townspeople. "What are you doing? Fluffles! Go get her! I command you!"

The chandelier spun more and more slowly and finally came to a stop. The squeaking ceased with one final click.

All was silent.

"I COMMAND YOU! FLUFFLES! ATTACK!" Bagalon shrieked.

The Fluffles leaned back, as if they had just woken from a peaceful dream on a picnic blanket.

Humungo let go of the rope. He looked at Emmaline on the chandelier. He looked at the calm Fluffles. He looked at the townspeople. Then he looked at Bagalon.

"Bagalon killed Queen Iliana," he shouted. "She said so herself!"

The townspeople turned and focused their eyes on Bagalon. The Fluffles sighed contentedly and closed their eyes. Several burped.

A chorus of "Bagalon killed Queen Iliana!" echoed throughout the Great Hall.

Queen Bagalon yelled, "FLUFFLES! ATTACK, YOU FOOLS! ATTACK!" Three or four Fluffles managed to stand, two picked up pitchforks, one even held his menacingly, but none, not a single Fluffle, attacked. Their eyelids drooped.

Bagalon took a step backwards. She held up her hands, palms out. "Now, wait a minute," she said. "Let's not be hasty. Remember, Pixoratta and Sofia are on trial here. They're the guilty ones! Not me!"

One by one, each townsperson made a fist with one hand and began to pound it in their other hand.

Bam!

Humungo's exceedingly large fist pounded his other hand.

Bam!

The Baker's fist sounded like a heavy bowl of dough being kneaded down.

Bam!

Bella's fist pounded as only a bodybuilder's could.

Dink!

The small man with the round glasses' fist—if you could even call it a fist—sounded like the gentle *clicking* of a grasshopper's wing. But what he lacked in fury with his tiny hands, he more than made up for with a fierce expression underneath his glasses.

The townspeople stepped forward.

Bam!

Bam!

Bam!

Bagalon stepped backwards.

Bam!

Bam!

Bam!

"This is just a misunderstanding," Bagalon said. She slipped her hand into the hidden pocket in the folds of her dress. But then a very odd thing happened. An exceptionally odd thing. Something I had never seen before nor do I hope I will ever see again happened. A Fluffle, relaxing on the floor, had just finished sucking the last bit of whipperoot candy, when he exploded.

Well, not exploded; not exactly. Not like a bomb explodes, or vinegar and baking soda explode out of a papier-mâché volcano, or even a balloon exploding when you give it a quick poke with a sharp pin. No, this Fluffle exploded more like a popcorn kernel explodes. He *popped*. His fur burst out—three, four, five times longer than it had been. It was soft and fuzzy. He flew through the air, shouting "Wheeee!" the entire way. Bits of yellow claws flew off like sparks from fireworks. A giant, flying puffball, he softly bounced off the ceiling and fell to the floor, not more than two steps from Humungo. The fuzzy Fluffle laughed like a baby who'd mastered the game of peekaboo.

"Hee hee! That was *awesome*! Hee! Hee! Hoo! Hoo!" he giggled.

The townspeople turned to look at the oddly fluffy puffball Fluffle lying on its back, smiling up at Humungo. The Fluffle couldn't stop laughing. *Hee hee hee! Hoo hoo hoo!*

Then another Fluffle popped, this time from the other side of the room, and *wahooed* over their heads. It fell in a gentle *poof* to the floor.

Queen Bagalon looked at the distracted townspeople and saw her opportunity. She pulled an empty hand from the secret pocket, stepped back, and ducked underneath the desk. She clawed around frantically until and found what she was looking for: a small metal ring embedded in the floor. She grabbed the ring and pulled. A trapdoor opened, exposing a tunnel underneath.

Like popcorn, another Fluffle, then another, then hundreds of Fluffles *popped* and *poofed* and ricocheted across the room. Large, puffy bundles of soft fur bounced off the walls, bumped into each other, and fell to the floor. Fluffles soon covered the floor, and, as more Fluffles popped, flew, and returned to earth, they covered the townspeople and Fluffles below them. Layer upon layer of laughing Fluffles filled the room from floor to ceiling with their fuzzy bodies. The room turned into a sea of giggling, wiggling, downy fuzz.

Standing on the platform, Dweezil looked at Weezil, and Weezil looked at Dweezil. Weezil appeared confused, perhaps concerned, unsure of what the purple candy was doing to him. He looked down at his hairless belly, and, as Dweezil watched, he popped. But not like popcorn. He didn't sail across the room. Only the few places where tufts of fur still clung to him like wet shoelaces popped. A naked body covered with long, fluffy sprouts of soft fur. He looked even more ridiculous than he had at the top of the stairs. Dweezil pointed at Weezil and burst out laughing. And then he also popped. Weezil pointed at Dweezil, and they both fell to the floor laughing hysterically.

Queen Bagalon dove into the tunnel and closed the trapdoor over her head. It was dark. She felt her way along the wall, crawling in the darkness on her hands and knees. She heard soft *pfff, pfff, pfff's* and *tee-hee-hee's* as Fluffles popped over her head. The tunnel ended in a solid wall, which, to the untrained eye, should have made her turn around and find another way out. However, Queen Bagalon slid her hand along the edge of the wall until she found a small catch. She pushed on it and a door slid sideways. On the other side of the doorway, a moist, stone hallway glowed green and sloped downhill. Bagalon slid through the opening and disappeared.

Back in the Great Hall the popping stopped. High on the chandelier sat Emmaline. The pile of Fluffles reached so high that Emmaline's feet touched the soft fur of the topmost Fluffle. It reminded her of sitting at the beach and wiggling her toes in the sand. She slid off the chandelier, wriggled, and squirmed through the giggling mass of fur until her feet found the floor. Emmaline crawled forward towards the cage on the platform.

In the cage, Pixoratta sat and drooled. Occasionally she twitched and yelled *"GARG!"* or *"MALARG!"* Her eyes darted about nervously, but her body lay slumped against the bars of the cage. Her greasy fur was so matted that she looked like an old mop used to clean one too many school cafeterias. Unfortunately, Pixoratta looked like a princess compared to Sofia. The young Fluffle lay in the center of the cage. She breathed in gasps, when she breathed at all. It sounded as if she were underwater, her breath gurgling up from a dank well.

Emmaline pulled on the door, hoping it was somehow unlocked, but, of course, it wasn't. "Help! Help me! Someone help! We need to help Pixoratta and Sofia! Someone unlock the cage!"

Humungo grabbed the bars and pulled with all his strength, but he might as well have been trying to push over a mountain. Bella grabbed another bar, and together, they both pulled, and grunted, and groaned, but the bars did not move.

Pixoratta twitched. "Schmarg. . . . Flarg schmarg. . . ."

"Don't worry, Pixoratta! We're going to get you out!"

"Flarg schmarg." Pixoratta closed her eyes. Her head fell sideways as if a puppeteer's cord had been cut.

"Move aside! Move aside!" exclaimed the Jeweler. She pushed through the mass of bodies, knocking Humungo and Bella out of the way. She carried her set of tools and bent down in front of the lock. She closed one eye and peered inside. The tip of her tongue stuck out of the left side of her mouth. "Hmm. . . . Looks like a Lemundo Lock . . .'" She pushed a thin metal needle into the lock and twisted a flat blade underneath it. "Very hard to pick . . . ." Her tongue slid out farther and her eyebrows scrunched together. "Very . . . hard . . . to . . . ." A *click* came from inside the lock and the Jeweler's face lit up. "But not for me." She pushed the door open.

Emmaline ran inside the cage and bent down. She sat down next to Sofia's body and put her friend's head in her lap. "No! No! No! No, you can't die, Sofia! Stay with us!" Tears streamed down Emmaline's face as she cradled Sofia in her arms and rocked the small Fluffle back and forth. Sofia's breathing came out in raspy spurts. She opened one

eye. There was no pupil; just a gray-green glow. Behind her, Pixoratta twitched, once, and lay still.

"Quick! Someone! Give them some whipproot candy! They need whipproot!"

Davinda saw one of the purple candies on the floor. She picked it up, held it between her fingers then bent down and reached for Sofia's mouth.

"STOP!" screamed a voice from behind them. "Don't give her that candy! Don't give either one of them *any* candy." The Baker hurried into the cage.

"But, they'll die if we don't give them the whipproot," said Emmaline.

"They'll *explode* if you give them that candy," said the Baker. "And I don't mean like popcorn, either. They're suffering from a mintussus overdose and if you give them a big bite of whipproot right now, well, the transition would be more than either of their small bodies could handle."

"But we need to do *something*."

"And we will. Don't you worry, Emmaline. Bring them back to my bakery. I'll make some tea."

Bella and Humungo scooped up the two Fluffles and carried their small bodies out of the cage. Sofia's arms hung limply by her side and swung with each step as they made their way through the crowd of Fluffles. The Baker raced ahead and put on a pot of water to boil, then laid out two large sacks of flour to act as beds for the dying Fluffles. As they reached the bakery, Pixoratta opened her eyes, reached out a small hand, grasped Emmaline by the elbow, and said, "Thargalarg, Emolarg. . . . Thargalarg."

Inside, the kettle whistled. The Baker set out two small cups, put a sprig of whipproot into each, and poured tea.

Recovering in the Bakery

IT HAD BEEN THREE WEEKS since the trial; three weeks since Emmaline, with the help of the townspeople, had put an end to Bagalon's treachery; three weeks since anyone had even seen Bagalon. The Baker had spent three weeks nursing Pixoratta and Sofia back to health, and the Fluffles, newly returned to their fluffy selves, spent three weeks repairing the damage they had done to the town. They whistled and sang and played harmless tricks on each other—nothing rude, mind you. Leading the effort were Dweezil and Weezil, two of the nicest, softest, snuggliest, hardest-working Fluffles you'd ever meet. Long into the night, well past the time other Fluffles had gone to bed, you would find both of them working away. Dweezil fixed the sign over the bakery and set doors back on their hinges. Weezil repaired fences, filled holes, painted, and even scrubbed the rust off of Humungo's anvil.

Inside the bakery, the Baker administered whipperoot to Pixoratta and Sofia. First, small sips of whipperoot tea; then tiny flakes of dried whipperoot sprinkled on toast; and finally, she gave them small pieces of whipperoot candy (made with dried whipperoot, not fresh) which her patients would suck on over the course of the day.

Pixoratta had recovered the fastest. She was almost one hundred percent back to her former self, if you didn't count her missing foot. Her majestic hair puffed and flowed when a breeze came through the window. Her white claws gleamed. The green and yellow had left her eyes. She didn't cough up, spit out, or drool sideways. And most happily, she was able to speak again. Her days of saying *flarg blarg snargetty snarg* had long passed.

Sofia did not fare as well, but she was improving. She sipped her tea and ate small bites of toast. Her lungs slowly cleared and only occasionally did she cough out anything green. Her voice was still quite raspy. Her fur looked a bit better; the grease had started to disappear. She still had a ways to go before her thick, luscious, Fluffle fur would return. Luckily, she never got violent or had trouble forming words like Pixoratta did.

Pixoratta sat in a chair and drank tea while Sofia lay on her sack of flour. Emmaline busied herself cleaning countertops.

"I know it isn't a very Fluffle-like thing to say," said Pixoratta, "but I wish we had been able to catch Bagalon. It upsets me to know she's out there, running around on the loose, doing who-knows-what."

After the trial, they had searched for Bagalon with the help of the townspeople. They had found the tiny metal ring in the floor and even managed to open the trapdoor to the secret tunnel below the platform. They had searched the tunnel end-to-end, found the hidden catch at the far end, and opened the hidden door at the far end. But after they slid through the opening into the dungeon hallway the trail went cold. No one had been able to figure out which way Bagalon had gone. The door to the dungeon was still locked, so she couldn't have come back up the hallway and escaped out through the castle. But there were no footprints, no fingerprints, no prints of any kind, indicating how she had escaped from the dungeon. She had, quite simply, vanished.

"I'm surprised none of the Fluffles was able to track her smell," said Emmaline.

"Track her what? Her smell?" said Pixoratta quite surprised. "Emmaline, what do you think we are? Bloodhounds?"

"No, I didn't mean that. It's just . . . well, it seemed to me when I was locked in the tower Dweezil and Weezil had very good noses. They sniffed around all the time. I think they smelled you, Sofia, hiding in my room."

Sofia smiled, happy to have that horrible chapter in her life behind her.

"Dweezil? A good smeller? I don't think so, Emmaline. Fluffles are notoriously *bad* smellers. I mean, er, what I mean is we smell bad, er not bad, but we don't smell good. What I mean is we don't smell *well*, that's what I mean. Fluffles can hardly tell the difference between a scented primrose and a frightened skunk."

"Really? I didn't know that."

"Fluffles have an amazing sense of feel," Pixoratta continued. "A Fluffle can sense every single hair on its body. If any slight breeze, landing insect, or even a speck of dust touches us, we can tell you exactly when it touched us, where it touched us, and which way it was going. We know how fast it was going and how much it weighs. We know everything about it, just from the way our fur moves." As if to demonstrate, Pixoratta ruffled her fur in waves around her body.

"Anyway, I guess that's why our sense of smell isn't so great. We make up for it with our sense of touch. Although, I do remember smelling things I hadn't smelled before."

"I guess that makes sense," said Emmaline. "Maybe when your fur was greasy from the mintussus, your noses made up for it."

Sofia rolled over on her side and fluffed up a bag of flour. "I can still smell. Not everything, but a lot," she said.

Pixoratta looked at her gently. "Oh, Sofia. Don't worry, dear. You're getting better. You still have a ways to go. Look at me. My fur is puffy and I can hardly smell a thing. You'll be just like me in no time."

"No, no. I know I'm getting better," said Sofia, "but I do smell you. Not in a bad way! You smell very nice, Pixoratta, as do you, Emmaline. But I smell the sacks of flour, and the salt and pepper in the storage closet. I smell the flowers outside and the grass and the river. Even Dweezil's sweat. He's probably building a new door because I smell sawdust, too."

Emmaline looked outside. Several blocks down the street, Dweezil stood on a porch cutting the final panel for a new front door.

"Anyway, maybe I could find Bagalon. You know, go back in the dungeon and sniff around some, before the mintussus wears off and my fur comes back."

"Oh, Sofia! Don't say that!" cried Emmaline. "Don't go back into that dungeon! Don't even think it!"

"I was just thinking maybe my nose is still good enough to find a clue."

Pixoratta twisted several chin hairs together and stuck out her bottom lip.

"I hadn't thought of that, Sofia. Do you think you could? I mean, you don't have to, no one's asking you, but . . . ."

"I could try, Emmaline. You'll be with me won't you?"

"Of course I'd go with you. But we don't need to. The guards are searching for Bagalon. I'm sure something will turn up."

"It's been weeks now. I doubt they'll find anything. We can do it, or at least try. If it is too scary, we'll come back."

The room got quiet. Sofia looked from Pixoratta to Emmaline and back again. Pixoratta slowly nodded her head and chewed on her bottom lip. Emmaline wore a mask of concern.

"Sofia, if you think you can, then I believe you can," said Pixoratta.

"Then we should go. Emmaline, are you ready?"

"You mean right now? You want to go right this second?"

"Yes. Before I lose any more of my sense of smell."

"Promise me you'll let me know if you need to turn back."

"I will."

The Search for Bagalon

EMMALINE AND SOFIA LEFT THE SAFETY and comfort of the bakery and walked slowly towards the castle. Fluffles greeted Sofia with a cheerful wave, happy to see her back on her feet again. But word spread very quickly that she and Emmaline were heading into the dungeon, and the cheerful waves turned into hushed voices which said things like: *What? She's going back into the dungeon? To search for Bagalon? She's out of her mind! I don't think she's fully recovered yet.* And, perhaps, the voices were right. One voice, however, was Humungo's, and his voice did not think the two were crazy. The Blacksmith had checked in on the girls every day for the past three weeks, making sure the Baker had everything she needed to nurse them back to health. When he heard they were going to the dungeon, he said, "Not without me, you're not," and fell in step with them. They walked to the castle, through the main hallway, down the side hallway, and arrived at the door to the dungeon entrance.

"You're sure you want to do this?" he asked Sofia.

"Yes. I'm sure."

Humungo pushed the door handle. The door swung open; the smell of rotting mintussus filled the hallway. Sofia and Emmaline both took a step back and covered their noses. They stood that way for a minute, letting their sense of smell get acclimated to the pungent aroma, then stepped into the dungeon hallway.

Sections of the walls glowed a bright green. Other sections, where the mintussus was starting to die and dry out, only emitted a pale green hue. A shimmer ruffled through Sofia's fur, like a lightning bolt rippling a still pond. Humungo reached out to steady her, but Sofia shook her head and stood straighter. They walked farther down the hallway until they came to a small hole halfway up the wall.

"This is where we think Bagalon crawled out," said Humungo. He held Sofia up to the opening, where she peered down the long, narrow tunnel, and, very faintly, made out the shaft of light coming through the trapdoor at the far end. Sofia breathed in. She closed her eyes and held her breath. Then she slowly let it out.

"She was here. I smell her perfume. Just barely, but she definitely was here." Sofia turned her head and sniffed, then sniffed again. "That way." She pointed down the hallway leading deeper into the dungeon.

They marched forward. Soon they arrived at the dungeon's only cell. Empty chains hung from the walls, specters of Sofia's and Pixoratta's ordeal. Dried mintussus clung to the wall and formed two silhouettes; the barrel in the corner was half full of water, its insides coated with a slimy residue—a mixture of mintussus, oil, and other nasty ingredients. Emmaline shuddered.

"We should keep going," said Emmaline. She smiled a tiny smile filled with sadness. She held her friend's hand as they silently walked down the hall, away from the horrid memories of Sofia's night in the cell.

They proceeded down another hallway deeper into the dungeon, then turned down a third hallway, then a fourth. At each intersection, Sofia sniffed, turned, and continued forward, always sure of her bearings. Then she stopped, confused, and looked around as if she had dropped something.

"I don't know what happened. I smell her perfume right up to this point, and then it disappears. It just stops. It's like she was swallowed up by the rock wall."

Humungo examined the wall. He bent down, stood up, and slid his meaty fingers along the stones, but found nothing. He tapped on the wall with his large fist. He thumped and pounded, up and down the wall.

"Wait! I think I heard something. Right there. Knock on the wall right there," said Emmaline. She pointed at a spot on the wall.

Humungo aimed a fist above Emmaline's hand and struck.

"Look at how the whole wall shakes when you hit it."

Humungo rolled his sleeve up to his elbow, pulled back his arm, and punched the stone wall as hard as he could. Bits of rock and splintered wood fell to the floor.

"This isn't stone! It's fake! Look at the wood underneath it. Stand back, ladies." Humungo rolled up his other sleeve, pulled both his fists back, and smashed the panel. A hidden door in the wall splintered into a thousand pieces. Behind it lay a dark, twisty passageway that smelled like rotten mushrooms. They followed the passageway and before long, Sofia caught a whiff of fresh air. The hallway became brighter and brighter. Light streamed in from an opening at the end of the tunnel, which let out onto a rock face on the side of Mount Gazooka. A narrow path clung to the side of the mountain. It was just wide enough to accommodate Emmaline or Sofia, but much too small to be comfortable for Humungo.

"Where are we?" said Sophia. "I've never seen this place before."

"This looks like the back side of Mount Gazooka," said Emmaline. "I've never seen it from this angle though."

Humungo looked over the side of the ledge. His knees shook. The cliff wall dropped straight down to Lake Gazombie, only partially named for the mountain it found itself next to and partially for the creatures that lived on its shores. (While the three were pretty certain of where they were, you, being a smart reader, would know *exactly* where they were—at the base of the path to the cave where Bagalon tricked Queen Iliana into taking her "permanent vacation.")

"I can't smell her anymore," said Sofia. "It's so windy. Her scent was probably blown away weeks ago."

"I bet she went up that path, up the side of the mountain. Don't you, Humungo?"

Humungo stepped back from the edge. His face was pale.

"Humungo? Are you OK?"

"Um. Yeah. Windy."

"No. Don't you think she must have gone up that path clinging to the side of the mountain?"

"Yeah. I just don't really like heights, if you know what I mean."

"It's not that bad. Look, there's lots of space to stand. See?" Emmaline danced around on the ledge.

"Maybe for you, Emmaline, but in case you haven't noticed, I'm a lot bigger than either of you. Heck, I'm bigger than both of you put together." Emmaline looked at the large blacksmith. It was true. He was bigger than anyone she had ever known. Even standing sideways, the front of his chest hung out over the edge of the ledge. "Maybe we should turn back."

Emmaline examined the path. It was narrow and crumbling. On one side, the mountain went one thousand feet straight up into the air. On the other side, it fell one thousand feet straight down to a watery grave.

"You can do it," said Sofia. "We'll help you."

Sofia casually stepped onto the path and held out a hand for the Blacksmith. He took the small Fluffle's hand and inched forward. Emmaline took his other hand and followed behind. Even with his back pressed flat to the wall, the toes of his shoes hung over the edge. He shuffled sideways, up the mountain path.

"You'll be fine. Just keep sliding one foot sideways then the next. You're doing great. Relax. You don't need to breathe so fast."

"And don't look down," said Sofia.

"There's no place for me to look *but* down!"

"Keep going. We're almost at that outcropping of rock. More than halfway. Just a little bit farther and we'll take a break."

The three slid farther up the mountain path and arrived at a small outcropping. Emmaline was afraid Humungo would burst into tears, but he leaned back on the large rock behind him and breathed a sigh of relief. She saw the veins in his neck pulse.

"See, that wasn't so bad, was it?"

"Yes. Yes it was," he replied. Once he had caught his breath and relaxed enough to take stock of his situation, he said, "This sure is a weird boulder. I can't imagine how a large rock like that didn't fall down the side of the mountain. It must've grown here or something."

Emmaline and Sofia sat on the edge of the outcropping. Their legs swung beneath them, over the thousand-foot drop.

"I just wanted to say thank you, Emmaline," she said, "you know, for saving my life. I'd be dead if it weren't for you."

"Not as dead as I'd be if it weren't for you. Remember when Dweezil tried to catch me in the cathedral? And when we crashed into that tree?"

"Yeah, I guess we're both pretty lucky, aren't we?"

They sat in the sunshine. The outcropping was warm under their legs and, quite frankly, they enjoyed just being outside after having spent the last three weeks lying on sacks of flour inside the bakery.

Emmaline stood up. "We should get going," she said. "I don't know how much farther up the mountain this trail goes."

Sofia stood up as well. "I guess you're right. We should—Do you smell that?"

"Smell what?"

"It smells like . . . ." Sofia sniffed and pinched her eyes together. "It smells like mothballs and velvet."

Queen Iliana's Statue

SOFIA SNIFFED THE GROUND and the rock wall. She climbed up Humungo's leg and sniffed the rock wall behind his arm. "I recognize that smell. It's familiar. It makes me think of the castle, and Queen Bagalon's bedroom, but not her bedroom, another room." Humungo moved sideways and Sofia pushed her nose into a small crack between the large boulder and the mountain's rocky face. She sniffed harder. "There's something in there. Behind the boulder. There's definitely something in there."

"Behind this rock?" asked Humungo.

"Yes. Definitely. There's definitely something back there." Sofia's nose twitched like a mouse.

Humungo stepped sideways, being sure to keep both feet on the outcropping. He bent his knees and pushed. The veins in his forehead and forearms bulged like iron ropes under his skin. He groaned and heaved. The rock swayed. He pushed again. It started to sway even farther, and then, with a mighty shove, the Blacksmith rolled the enormous boulder off the edge of the cliff. He watched it bounce one thousand feet down the cliff face until it crashed with a silent splash into Lake Gazombie. Behind Humungo, a cave, which had been blocked by the boulder, opened its mouth to them.

Sofia scurried into the cave on her hands and knees. Her nose traced the ground as she sniffed furiously. Small rocks littered the cave's dirt floor. When she exhaled, clouds of gray dust swirled in front of her nose. Emmaline stepped into the cave. She let her eyes adjust to the dim light. In the back of the cave, she saw a massive stone chair carved from a single piece of solid rock. Sitting in the chair, carved from the same block of stone, was a statue of Queen Iliana. Her stone hands clasped stone armrests. Her eyes were closed, peaceful, and covered with a layer of dust. A spider's web formed a lace triangle between her crown, shoulder, and neck. Her skin looked like dried leather stretched over sticks.

"Oh my goodness! Humungo! Over here! It's Queen Iliana's body!"

Humungo stooped down through the entryway and joined Emmaline in the back of the cave. Sofia stood up next to them. "This is Queen Iliana?" Sofia said.

"*Was* Queen Iliana," corrected Humungo.

Humungo bent down on one knee. He clasped his hands together in front of his chest, bowed his head, and said a prayer.

"She looks so peaceful," said Emmaline. She ran a finger down one of the Queen's sleeves, leaving a fingertip-sized trail of dust behind. Her hand traced over the ornate lace at the end of the cuff, then down the back of Queen Iliana's hand. Her skin was scratchy and cold and had a brittleness to it that made Emmaline fear it would flake off. Emmaline dropped her head. Tears rolled down her cheeks.

Humungo put an arm around Emmaline's shoulder. "We should go back to the castle, get a casket, and get some people to help—"

"Look! Humungo! Emmaline! Look!" Sofia pointed at the Queen's face.

Emmaline raised her eyes and looked at Queen Iliana's marble face. The statue's eyes opened, closed, and opened again, two blue orbs surrounded by a sea of gray. Dust fell from eyelashes and rolled down the statue's face, neck, and dress.

"Queen Iliana?"

The Queen turned her head slowly to the side, like an automaton, then to the other side, and finally returned to the center. Her mouth opened, as if to speak, then closed. Large swatches of dust rolled down her sunken cheeks and off chapped lips. She opened her mouth again and spat out a small piece of pink candy. When she finally spoke her voice sounded very far away, a faint vibration carried on a small current of air from deep within her.

"Emma . . . Emmaline? Is that you?"

"Yes! Yes! It's me! You're alive! I can't believe it! You're alive!" Emmaline jumped up and threw her arms around Queen Iliana. Emmaline's tears streamed down her cheeks and turned to mud on Iliana's neck. Humungo grabbed both of them and gave them a tremendous hug. Then he reached out his arm and hugged Sofia as well.

"And who is this?" Queen Iliana asked, looking at Sofia.

"Queen Iliana, this is my friend, Sofia. She's a Fluffle."

"A Fluffle! You don't say! Oh, I'm so excited to finally have the pleasure of meeting an honest-to-goodness Fluffle. So nice to meet you, Sofia." The Queen paused and looked down at her right arm. "Hmm. It seems I can't move my arm. Otherwise, I would shake your hand right now. Oh, this *is* embarrassing." She wiggled a finger at the end of her arm, but otherwise, nothing twitched. "My legs don't seem to want to move either. How long have I been asleep, Emmaline? It's pretty dark in here. Makes it hard to keep track of the time."

"You've been gone almost two years," said Emmaline.

"Two years! Why, that's impossible! Don't be silly! Two years! Emmaline! How absurd! And don't you try to prank me either, Humungo. I see you over there with that ridiculous look on your face. How about you help me stand up, instead? Two years! Well, I never! That's the silliest thing I've ever heard!"

Humungo bent over, put his giant hands underneath Queen Iliana's frail body, and lifted her into the air like a pile of dry twigs wrapped in a velvet dress.

A Queen-shaped silhouette of dust remained on the throne where Iliana had sat.

The Return of the Queen

HUMUNGO CARRIED QUEEN ILIANA out of the cave, onto the rock outcropping, and side-stepped down the mountain path. He carried her through the secret passageway, past the secret doorway (now broken to splinters), past the cell, up the hallway, and into the castle proper. But instead of going to her bedroom to recover, as Humungo suggested, Queen Iliana insisted on visiting her subjects. A royal carriage was summoned; the four climbed in and the driver *click-clicked* to the horses. It was quite a group: Humungo, who filled up most of the carriage by himself (the carriage leaned to his side); Sofia, small and petite, with a touch of oil in her fur; Emmaline, hugging the Queen close to her; and Queen Iliana herself, a gaunt, dusty apparition of her former self.

As they rode through town, Queen Iliana waved at the shocked townspeople. "My goodness! The kingdom does look spectacular! Look at all the new doors and fences and windows. And all the Fluffles working side by side with the townspeople, planting gardens and fixing roofs. This is absolutely wonderful! It's so nice to see everyone getting along. I've never seen the kingdom look so good! Bagalon really has done a *magnificent* job running things while I was away! Where is Bagalon? I really must thank her."

Humungo, Sofia, and Emmaline looked at each other, glancing quietly from face to face, until all three burst out laughing.

"My heavens! What is wrong with you? What on earth are you laughing about? And where is Bagalon?"

Emmaline leaned her head out of the window and asked the coachman to stop. He pulled back on his reins and the horses slowed in front of a building with a sign over the door which read DELICIOUS, HOMEMADE BREAD, CAKES, PIES and PASTRY! Through an open window, Emmaline saw Dweezil hard at work in the kitchen making a fresh batch of pies.

"That, Queen Iliana, is quite a story; one I think that would best be told over a raspberry scone and a cup of tea. And lucky for you, I happen to know someone who makes the world's best whippleroot tea."

The End

Postface

Why are you still reading this? Did you not see "The End" written on the last page? It was only one page ago. A smart reader, like yourself, would have read that and thought, *Hmm. . . . I must be at the end. It's over. I can go to sleep now*, if you were reading in bed; or, *Hmm. . . . I can go back to the dinner party*, if you were hiding in a bathroom and reading this instead of small-talking at people you don't know and don't really care to; or, *Hmm. . . . I really wish I brought a parachute instead of this book*, if you happen to be reading it while skydiving, which I assume you are.

Well, if you may recall, I warned you this was a terrible story with a horrible ending and you shouldn't read it. And yet, here you are, even reading the extra pages at the end as you plummet from the sky to your imminent demise. So, let me be quick. I assume you don't have much time.

Let me guess—you're reading this page to find out what happened to Queen, er, I mean, *former Queen*, Bagalon. After all, she was a horrible creature and in every fairy tale the horrible creature always gets it in the end. Maybe they're eaten by a dragon or slain by a prince or die from a peanut allergy. It doesn't really matter, just as long as they croak before it says, "The End."

No one knows what happened to Bagalon. She did sneak out of the Great Hall, through the secret tunnel, and likely climbed over Mount Gazooka. I did the climb myself. It's hard, but not impossible. She did not plummet to her death down the side of the mountain. I dove to the bottom of Lake Gazombie and found nothing, no clothes or bones anywhere. So, no one—not me, not you, not Sofia or Emmaline, nor even the small man with the round glasses—has any idea of Bagalon's whereabouts. This is real life and not a fairy tale. You will just have to learn to accept it.

However, I do promise, if I ever do find out what happened to Bagalon, the very moment I find out, I will write you and let you know.

Now, without delay, I suggest you glide through the air over to your skydiving friends and see if any of them happens to have an extra parachute you could borrow, since this book will do little to slow your fall. Otherwise, this will be both the end of the book and the end of you.

I can think of worse ways to go.

About the Author

Born and raised in Sumskwut Gulch, JJ McGeester is the ninth child of Rufus and Edna McGeester, who never really noticed him on the farm. As a present on his seventh birthday, JJ received two gerbils—both boys—until Gerry the Gerbil gave birth to eight healthy gerblings. Always thinking, JJ started gerbil-farming, raising world-class gerbils for circuses around the globe. Famous gerbils like "Ferdinando del Fuego" who holds the world record for the longest motorcycle jump through fire performed by a gerbil, or "Aquana the Breathless" who once swam underwater from the North Pole to the South Pole and back again, or "Camella" who watched ninety-nine episodes of "Party Gerbils of St. Tropez" without having to take a single bathroom break.

About the Illustrator

JJ McGeester also did the drawings for this book, which is why, when discussing the artwork of the book over a cup of coffee and some treats with your best friend, you might have remarked, "the drawings look like they were done by a gerbil farmer from Sumskwut Gulch."

And you'd be correct.

www.jjmcgeester.com